Deliverance for Duncan

Deliverance for Duncan

Ruth Kuepfer

For additional copies or information
about the book contact:

Chai with Ruth
8626 Mission Home Road
Free Union, VA 22940

© July 2008 Ruth Kuepfer

ISBN: 978-0-615-21655-3

Printed by:

Carlisle Printing
OF WALNUT CREEK Ltd.

2673 Township Road 421
Sugarcreek, OH 44681

Contents

Part One

Destitute

Anticipate some African phrasing in conversation.

chapter one

The Street Urchin

D UNCAN SHIVERED IN HIS RAGS AS HE AWAKENED IN A CRUMBLING MUD
hut in Nyalenda, Kenya. The season of the long rains made nights
chilly without a blanket. Ten-year-old Duncan never knew where he would
find shelter. Last night he and his friend, Aloyce, had bedded down with a
poor family of five, who begrudgingly allowed them a small space on their
reed mat.

But it's better than being at home, Duncan thought. Those awful days
after *Baba's* (father's) funeral made everyone in our family glum. Folks
acted scared when they said he died of *chira*. (a curse) Duncan remembered
Mama's fearful eyes as she explained that the curse of *chira* is what made him
get thin and die.

Duncan remembered how skinny his *baba* had looked, lying there in a
rough wooden coffin. *That's not really* Baba, he had thought. Baba *had mean
black eyes. Now he looks like he is sleeping.* The funeral drums had beaten
deep into the night as family and friends sat up for the wake. Not until after
a midnight supper did he catch a few winks of sleep.

After the funeral, Uncle Macharius had come to visit Mama and spend
the night with her. He would need to come back at least once a year according
to Luo tribal custom. This is what their tribe called wife inheritance--Uncle

Macharius took care of Mama now. *They didn't want me anymore after my sister was born*, Duncan thought, *sometimes that makes me glad I decided to run away to the wild, free life of the streets.*

Duncan remembered one of the terrible tongue-lashings he'd often received from his mother. On this particular day, he had innocently planted a certain type of tree, breaking one of the Luo customs.

"You will die from *chira*, just like your *baba*! The spirits will finish your life!" she screamed. Then she beat him with her wooden stick she used to stir *ugali*. (a thick corncake) Duncán cringed, for he'd been told if someone were beaten with the *ugali* spoon, he would die from *chira*. *So she wants to inflict the curse on me herself*, he worried. Then the stick broke, and Uncle Macharius came on the scene.

"What have you done! You not only give anger to your ancestors, but must you also destroy your mama's *ugali* spoon?" *As if he doesn't care that now I'll die of* chira, thought Duncan bitterly. In a terrible rage, Uncle had caned him until he could hardly walk.

Now as Duncan lay there in the slums, he resolved, *I'm never going back home again!* He scratched his shaved head, stretched, and sat up. Poking his head out the door of the crumbling mud hut, he gazed in awe as the sunrise spun swirls of gold and pink around the sky.

Squatting in the doorway, Duncan reached automatically for the glue bottle hidden in the depths of his rags. His buddy Aloyce was still sleeping with his glue jar dangling from a ragged coat sleeve. Duncan wished his friend would wake up. Bored, he took a long sniff of glue, waiting for the euphoria that would follow. When he had inhaled enough, his eyes went out of focus. He began skipping around, oblivious to how silly he looked. He chanted phrases that made no sense. All too soon, the glorious feeling would drift away and he would feel sick.

Duncan took another drag on his glue bottle. Then he shook Aloyce. "Get up! Let's go to the market!" he said in Swahili, the language used by street boys. The older boy grunted and made a face. Duncan grabbed for Aloyce's glue bottle with a silly laugh, hoping to lure him onto the streets. At this, the other boy sat up jerkily. Seeing his glue bottle being snatched away, Aloyce lunged at Duncan.

"You madman! Give that to me!" he croaked, now thoroughly awake. When Duncan returned his glue, Aloyce pretended to settle down for another snooze. Duncan shook him firmly, but Aloyce merely rolled over and refused to cooperate.

Duncan wandered out of the slum district into town as his euphoria began to wear off. He felt the familiar nausea and tried not to retch. Cuddling his glue bottle, he took another sniff.

Other street boys began to emerge from under various store awnings. Last night the rain had blown in from Lake Victoria, and most of the street campers had gotten a little soggy. Undeterred, they wandered along the streets. Soon they were digging in a garbage can for their breakfast, hoping some leftovers had been missed in the previous night's rummaging.

Duncan jumped up and trotted over to Maria's Cafe, which the boys had dubbed the Shade Tree Hotel. This tiny restaurant had a tin roof built around a giant shade tree. Two of his friends were quarreling over some stale *ugali* they found in a garbage can. Soon the boy with the runny nose had stuffed the whole thing in his mouth and the other boy stood enraged, calling him names. The greedy urchin finished gobbling the *ugali* before taking a drag on his glue bottle. Duncan shrugged and peered into the garbage can.

"Any more food in here?" he asked the boy with the runny nose.

The victor of the fight mumbled, "I don't think so. You know most people who eat here finish their food." Yes, Duncan knew. He had heard of a land called America where white people ate half their meal and threw the rest away. He figured he could live off the fat of the land if he visited their garbage sites. Duncan didn't bother dirtying his hands in the cafe's refuse. He hurried back to check up Aloyce, hoping his best friend had finally decided that it was morning.

But no, he was still snoozing, trying to draw some warmth from a gunny sack and the bumpy reed mat. Duncan sighed with exasperation.

"It's time you wake up," Duncan barked. "Are you sick?"

Dark, haunted eyes opened, and Aloyce moaned, "Yes, I'm sick. I feel cold, wet, and hungry. Did you find some food?"

"No. If you'd get up and go with me to beg at market like we usually do, maybe you wouldn't feel so sick. We could drink some nice, warm porridge."

Sighing, Aloyce folded his burlap sack and stuffed it away in a crevice. He followed Duncan as they savored the sensation of the sun's warm fingers beginning to thaw out the dampness of the night. Duncan figured it would get pretty hot this morning before it rained again in the afternoon. For such are the days of the long rains.

The Jubilee Market teemed with life as traders began spreading out their fresh produce. The colorful array of fruits and vegetables made Duncan's mouth water. With Aloyce's taller form looming behind him, he trotted over to the banana vendor. She frowned at the sight of two ragged street boys, but Duncan was too hungry to notice. He made sure his glue bottle was well-hidden in the folds of his grimy sleeve.

"I'm cold, wet, and hungry," he said. "Give me a banana! I'm your first customer!" She raised her eyebrows.

"They are ten shillings a bunch for my first customer." Even Aloyce had to admit that was a good price.

Yet Duncan went on whining, "I have no money! Just give!" His face was so woe-begone and forlorn that the Banana Mama's chubby cheeks relaxed into a toothless grin.

"All right. Five shillings each," she agreed. The two beggars counted the bananas, and figured she was charging about a half shilling each. Yet they both knew they could not eat bananas today, for neither owned even a half shilling at the moment. Their faces fell, and they began to walk away. Then they heard a cackle behind them and saw two chubby hands holding out a small banana to each boy. The old woman felt sure she would be blessed with high sales today because of her good deed. Duncan and Aloyce grabbed their booty without a "thank-you" and began gobbling their meager breakfast. After that, they wandered around to look for food or money. Soon Aloyce was carrying around a white lady's basket for her--they usually paid well. Duncan found a rich Indian to beg from, but received only a shilling.

In the early afternoon, they each went to buy a gourd of runny *nyuka*. (thin corn gruel) Duncan watched as a mother fed some to her three-month-old baby. The infant hollered, but the mom kept on spooning the cornmeal substance into the baby girl's mouth, pinching shut the little nose so she would be forced to swallow. The baby gurgled and spit out the nyuka, but her mother spooned it back in again.

Duncan wolfed down his own nyuka while Aloyce savored his, trying to make it last longer. They liked nyuka better with sugar, but this stuff had enough salt and a hint of lemon, so it was pretty good.

Just then Duncan spied a white lady in a car beside the street. Leaving Aloyce behind, he rushed over to the car, thinking he might beg a shilling from the white people. As soon as he approached, all the car windows went up. *They think I'm a horrid thief*, he huffed to himself. *Of course, I don't mind stealing, but I'm not poison.* Pressing his nose against the glass, he saw three children; the youngest looked about his age. He stretched out his hands in entreaty, a pleading look on his face. The oldest rolled down his window a crack and barked, "Go home to your mama!"

"I have no mama," he whimpered. The white children tried to reply to him, but his English was limited enough that he did not understand.

"Give me a shilling!" he begged. He knew a few key phrases in English. Sometimes he would pretend to cry and even make tears come, but before he could begin his act, the little girl his age caught his attention. She was saying something in his language--what was it? He asked her in Luo to repeat what she had said.

"Begging is wrong," she replied in his language. Duncan sniffed and threw back his shoulders. How else could he survive? They didn't understand! Just then, the white woman came with Aloyce in tow, carrying two laden baskets. Duncan ignored Aloyce and put on a long face.

"Give me bread," he pleaded. Smiling, the woman pointed to a loaf of yellow sweet bread. Then she pointed to his bulging sleeve, but Duncan hid his arm behind his back.

"Give me glue. I give you bread." She reached for the precious glue bottle that Duncan felt he could not give up. Why did she want glue anyway? "Glue is bad. Give me glue. Glue is bad. I give you good bread."

Duncan was put on the spot. *So glue is bad and bread is good? That makes sense. I know glue gives me a headache and makes me vomit sometimes after the high feeling wears off.* He had been hungry for so long that eating had become a matter of only staving off the hunger pangs a little. To think of a whole loaf of bread!

Aloyce had run off somewhere to help carry baskets for someone else. Duncan double-checked. No one was watching. Slowly, the little glass jar came up out of his tattered sleeve. He looked at the glue, counting the cost. Was it worth it? He saw the pleading look in her eyes, and then he knew. She didn't want his glue. She cared about him. Never before had someone truly cared about Duncan.

He relinquished the glue into her outstretched hands, and received the precious loaf of bread. The white lady's eyes watered. Duncan didn't know if she was crying, or if the fumes from the glue jar bothered her. He looked away. Her blue eyes compelled him to turn back again. She asked in Luo, "Where do you live?" Duncan's eyes widened. *She actually bothered to learn our tribal dialect!* Most *wasungu* (white people) just learn Swahili, the national language.

"Nyalenda," he replied. Her eyes softened, as though she were thinking of the thousands who were crammed in Kisumu's little slum of Nyalenda.

Unexpectedly, the lady said, "Why don't you come to the orphanage. It's a place for children with no mommy or daddy."

"Where?" asked Duncan. His heart skipped a beat at the thought of someone to love him.

"Not far from Moi Stadium," she replied. "Come! I live there, too. I will be your new Mama." Duncan's memories of a mama weren't very good. This lady would never be his mama! But at least she cared about him. The white lady opened the car door for him, and motioned for the smallest girl to move over. Duncan hesitated.

In hushed tones, he conferred with his buddy. "What do you think? Is the orphanage a good place to go?"

Aloyce had lived at a children's home before it shut down, releasing him once more to the streets. He replied, "There is usually food and maybe new clothes. They will give you some schooling. But you will not be free to roam the streets with us."

Duncan counted the cost. "Will you come, too?" he asked finally.

Aloyce shrugged. "They did not ask me to come," he replied. He didn't look much taken with the idea.

The promise of food and clothes seemed attractive, especially education–so dear to an African's heart. But having someone who really cared for him was what persuaded him to go at last. Leaving his friend and the dreary life on the streets, he climbed uncertainly into the white lady's car. *What lies ahead?* Duncan wondered. *What will this orphanage really be like?*

chapter two
The Orphanage

As they jostled over the ruts and potholes on the road to the orphanage, Duncan began to wonder if he had made the right decision. The white lady seemed to like him, but her children acted like little terrors. The pale-skinned girl beside him made horrible faces at him, while the older boy held his nose and snickered. *Why are they making fun of me?* Duncan wondered.

Soon the white mama slowed to a stop in front of a huge, run-down building swarming with other black children. Suddenly, Duncan felt lonely for Aloyce. Would he be able to make new friends? He determined to try.

As they walked over to the building, Duncan's stomach rumbled. "Where is food?" he asked. "I am very hungry."

"You may call me 'Mama June,'" the white lady said. "Come. I will see if there are any leftovers in the kitchen.

As he trailed her into the sparse kitchen, a few orphans stared at him. However, most of them continued their game of soccer, for it was not unusual to see yet another ragged boy arriving at their home.

After Duncan had devoured some cold *ugali*, his stomach felt quite comfortable. Next, Mama June filled a tub with cool water from the well and set it in the sun. After it had warmed for about an hour, she gave Duncan a bar of soap. "Take a bath," she told him, and went away to some business of her own.

A short while later, a boy Duncan's size brought him a used, but clean set of clothing. "My name is Justus," he said. "Who are you? Are you a street boy?" he asked curiously. "Did you sniff glue?"

Duncan waited until he pulled his head through the T-shirt, then said, "I am Duncan. My *baba* is dead, and my mamma didn't want me after she was inherited by my uncle. After that, I went to live on the streets." Somehow it seemed natural to tell Justus his history.

The other boy's eyes widened. "Are you a glue sniffer?"

"No," Duncan lied. He didn't think it was any of Justus' business. But he could tell Justus didn't really believe him because he saw his new friend searching the recesses of his discarded clothes. Duncan sighed and admitted, "I gave my glue to Mama June. I'm going to leave sniffing glue." Justus nodded as if it were an everyday occurrence to see someone giving up an addiction so quickly.

Justus and Duncan became inseparable. Duncan was glad to have someone to introduce him to his new surroundings and show him how things were done at the orphanage. The two ate together, slept together, and studied together.

Duncan had never attended school of any kind before. Since he was still young, sniffing glue had not fried his brain completely. Still, he found it harder to learn than Justus, who had never sniffed glue. A sea of black boys and girls sat on crude benches and copied the lesson into their notebooks from the blackboard painted on the wall.

Before Duncan did anything else, he needed to learn how to hold a pencil. The schoolmaster placed a slender stick in Duncan's hand and tried to show him how to use it. Obligingly, Duncan pressed down as he had seen the others do. PPPinggg! To his astonishment, the stick was now in two pieces! Embarrassed, he picked them up amidst a backdrop of snickers.

He looked up, and saw Mama June's two children giggling behind their hands--the very ones who had made fun of him on the way to the orphanage. *They are laughing me, but I think sometimes they also make mistakes,* Duncan tried to comfort himself.

He felt a light tap on his arm. "Don't worry," Justus whispered. "Those proud white children are orphans like us. They don't have their father." Duncan smiled triumphantly.

The two little white children were full of mischief and liked to play tricks on Duncan and Justus. One day, when the *wasungu* (white people) knew that the two boys had snuck to the kitchen to pilfer a forbidden snack, they ran to fill gallon pails with water and crouched on the overhanging roof above the doorway. As soon as Duncan walked out the door, a torrent of water descended on his head. Justus was likewise doused.

"Aaaiii!" they shouted, shocked by the chilly wetness. At first they were quite enraged and called the white children all kinds of names. But when they heard Mama June's children giggling, the two boys joined in their laughter when they realized the water actually felt good. Before too many days had passed, the children became friends.

One day while Duncan was in line waiting for his allotment of food, he saw the cook scrape the bottom of the large pot before he even got there.

"Aaaiii!" he gasped. "The food is finished."

Justus, who was right behind him, replied, "Sometimes the food is not enough. Then we have to go and beg." His face bristled with the injustice of it. The food shortage surprised Duncan, for Mama June had promised there would be plenty of food at the children's home. Yet life had handed him so many disappointments that he just took it in stride.

"Where did you go to beg when you lived on the streets?" the children asked Duncan. "Can you show us a good place? We are tired of begging at the places we're used to going."

"You mean you go on the streets to beg when there's not enough food?" Duncan asked, surprised. They nodded, clamoring for him to show him the spots where the most generous people were.

Duncan led the hungry children out to his old begging haunts. They told Mama June they were going to swim in Lake Victoria, but snuck out to the streets. Justus seemed humiliated to be seen begging, but Duncan was in his glory. This was the life he knew best.

Even though Duncan enjoyed his new life, he struggled with his addiction to the glue bottle. "I must have some glue today, even one sniff," he agonized to his friend one morning. Justus' midnight skin seemed even blacker as his eyes shone out large and white.

"You said you were going to leave glue sniffing. Now you must keep your word. It's not good for you; it's best you can't get any." This was a battle with which Justus could not sympathize. Duncan shook his head with frustration.

Some time later, Duncan decided to try and find Aloyce the next time he went to beg on the streets. He was lonely for his familiar crony and yearned for a sniff of glue. Why had he given up his wild freedom for the stifling security of this orphanage anyway?

The next day a man pulled a cart of dried tilapia fish over to the orphanage–a generous donation. The children need not go begging for several days. Yet his ravenous craving led Duncan out to the streets. *Somehow I must find a glue bottle,* he agonized.

He searched for Aloyce at Jubilee Market, and waved at the big mama who had given them bananas on the long-ago day he had gone to the orphanage. However, she didn't seem to recognize him. Aloyce was nowhere to be seen. Duncan looked high and low in all of their old haunts, but couldn't find his friend. What had happened to Aloyce?

Then he saw him--but was this Aloyce? He remembered a small boy with a shaved head, but this boy was tall, shaggy, and filthy! He was obviously high on glue and skipped around, muttering like a mad-man. He saw Duncan, but no gleam of recognition dawned in his bloodshot eyes.

"Aloyce!" Duncan called. "Do you know me?" His former buddy just gave a whoop, oblivious to anything but the euphoria he was experiencing. At that moment, Duncan's desire for glue melted away. *I escaped becoming like Aloyce when I went to the orphanage,* he realized. *I'm glad I am not now a shaggy street boy, high on glue. I want to become a dependable man,* he determined.

Duncan returned to the orphanage with his heart full of gratitude to Mama June. He decided to try harder to please her. He was determined to study the concepts taught by the school master more diligently, even though sniffing glue had left him a slow learner.

One night, as Duncan and Justus were lying on the reed mat they shared as a bed, Justus whispered, "Did you know that sometimes people take orphans into their homes as their own children? They choose the orphan they like the most."

Duncan sat up with a start. "Yes, I noticed two of the orphans from here went to live with a kind man and woman. It would be nice to have real parents," he admitted to his friend. "I know Mama June is kind, but she can't be a good mom to all of us. Sometimes I still feel like an orphan."

"You know what, sometimes I feel like that too. Me, I want someone to take me as their son. But I'm not cute, and the cute ones get picked first," Justus lamented.

"No, you're not cute--you are like a long stalk of sugar cane," teased Duncan. Justus clubbed him back playfully, and soon they were wrestling on the floor. Mama June was making her evening rounds, and caught them.

"Hey! This is the time to sleep, not fight," she admonished. The two subsided into smothered laughter as they obediently took their places on the reed mat.

In the months that followed, Duncan often felt overly restricted by all the rules and longed for the free life he'd known on the streets. Yet the image of Aloyce and his dread-locks would return, and he decided to wait it out until someone would adopt him. Surely there must be a family out there who would take him as their very own.

Then one day a Land Cruiser of white girls drove up to the orphanage. The children all clustered curiously around the new-comers. Were they visitors for Mama June? No, it seemed that they had come to see the orphans themselves!

Everyone pushed to get a lollipop when the girls began to pass out candy. The *wasungu* even spoke a little Luo and smiled lovingly at them. After playing with the babies in the nursery, some of the girls began setting up a wooden stand. They put a felt-covered board on it, and covered it with colorful felt figures.

All the children sat and listened with rapt attention to the Bible story which was translated into the Luo language. Duncan had heard Bible stories before, but they had never come alive as now when he could picture them on the flannel board! Yet he couldn't help but wish the girls had come to adopt some orphans, maybe even adopt him.

That night he prayed his first prayer. "Dear God, please help someone to 'dopt me. Put me in a home with a mamma and *baba*. Amen." If Duncan had known what the future held, he may not have prayed to leave the orphanage.

chapter three

A New Home

ONE BRIGHT TUESDAY WHEN FOOD WAS SCARCE AT THE ORPHANAGE, Duncan and Justus crept out to the streets once again to beg with the others. The market, Duncan's favorite spot, teamed with life as usual. Those fortunate enough to own vehicles could hardly find a space to park, and people of varying shapes and sizes milled around. Inside the market, Duncan's keen ears picked up Swahili, Luo, and English, even though everyone was jabbering at once. The three years Duncan had spent at the orphanage had treated him well. He was growing tall and muscular with a sharp wit about him.

He spotted a big Luo mama who was struggling to carry a bulging basket. *She must be rich to buy so much food*, he thought. *Or maybe she is having a* duka. (small booth-like store) "Here, I will carry for you the basket," he offered in the vernacular.

Her eyes lit up. "Thank you," she said, handing over the brightly woven basket with its vivid assortment of fruits and vegetables. He lugged it along as she went down the aisles bargaining for produce. As she filled the second basket, he did double duty with a basket slung over each sturdy arm.

After he had carried the lady's food to a *matatu* (public transportation vehicle), she gave him five shillings. He grinned from ear to ear and scampered off to buy some porridge for his breakfast. Something about that lady's kind manner appealed to him. She had actually thanked him for carrying the load as though he mattered as a person.

Justus hadn't needed to work, for he had begged ten shillings from a wealthy Asian. Together they drank their thin porridge, then used Justus' extra five shillings to buy a meat pastry. Happy with their morning's success, they went for a brief swim before returning to the orphanage.

The next Tuesday, even though the orphanage cook was boiling beans for lunch, Duncan wanted to go to market. *Maybe that mama needs me to carry her baskets again,* he thought, *because she said Tuesday was the day she did her shopping in Kisumu.* Sure enough, she was there. She seemed to recognize him, for she beckoned him to come and help with her baskets.

Thus began Duncan's tradition of helping Mama Dolphine, as she was called, on the days she shopped at market. "I am buying this food for my *duka,*" she had explained. Duncan had told Justus of his weekly rendezvous, but the other boy just shrugged. He didn't understand why Duncan thought he must continually help this Mama Dolphine with her market shopping.

Once Mama Dolphine asked, "You aren't a regular street boy, are you?"

Duncan shamefacedly confessed, "No, I live at an orphanage. Sometimes we don't have enough food, so we go to beg on the streets. But I like to come and help you." She smiled.

Because Duncan was helping Mama Dolphine from a heart of love, he did not always require payment. However, whenever he let her know the food was scarce that day, she either slipped him some extra shillings or treated him to a meal at the hotel. In this way, their friendship thrived as the months passed.

One day after Duncan had carried the baskets to the *matatu* for her, they chatted for a few minutes as was their custom.

Mama Dolphine wondered, "Duncan, do you like it at the orphanage?"

Duncan shook his head. "Not really, but it is a better thing than living on the streets. I think Mama June loves me, but she can't do for me like a real mother would. We are too many."

"I love you very much. Why don't you come and stay with me? You will be like my real son. My husband is old, and my daughters have gone to cook (got married). I have one son remaining at home. We would be happy to welcome you in our *dala*." (circle of huts that make up a Luo home)

Duncan's eyes glowed. "I'm seeing this as good. I agree to come as your son. Why don't you talk to Mama June from the orphanage?" Mama Dolphine nodded, and arranged to come to the orphanage the following Monday.

That night as Justus was drifting off to sleep, Duncan remarked to him, "You know, I thought Mama June loved me when she brought me to the orphanage. Yet she doesn't have enough time to be a real mother to me because she has much work. Some days I barely see her. We have our caretakers and teachers, but it's not the same."

Justus drowsily murmured, *"Eee." (yes)*

Duncan continued earnestly, "It's not the same as a real home would be, with a mother and father. My own home was not so good, but most of the other boys whose parents died speak of a good life in a real home. I know life could be better." He brushed the tears away impatiently. The tremor in his voice caused Justus to sit up, sleep forgotten.

Duncan went on. "You remember me talking about this mama I met at the market whose name is Dolphine? She is my friend, and I like to carry her market basket every Tuesday. I hope she takes me home with her sometime." His excitement was unmistakable.

Justus bristled. "What are you saying?" he demanded. "Are you having a plan behind my back? Why did you not speak of this to me before?"

Duncan sighed. "I would not be leaving you alone. There are a hundred other children here." He tried to reassure his friend while his own lip quivered at the thought of leaving.

"I don't want a hundred children. I want you to stay with me!" The last note was high-pitched. "Is this woman Dolphine going to take you home with her, really?" Justus asked tearfully.

Duncan replied, "I think so. She will talk to Mama June on Monday. I think that Mama June loves me a bit, but Mama Dolphine loves me much more, and she promised to spend time with me like a real mother." His heart thrilled with the security his new mama's love would bring to him. He would feel more like any other normal boy with a mama and a home. But it would mean leaving Justus. Was it worth it?

"You will leave when? I have how much more time to spend with you?" Justus asked.

"I don't know," Duncan replied tremulously. Another tear slipped down his cheek at the thought of leaving his friend behind. The two boys tried to hide their tears in the darkness. What different lives they were destined to lead!

True to her word, Mama Dolphine visited the orphanage director, Mama June. The black lady gazed steadily into Mama June's blue eyes as she requested, "I want to take my friend Duncan with me to my home as my son."

Mama June asked Duncan, "Do you want to go with Dolphine? Do you think she will give you a good home?"

Duncan swallowed as he thought of leaving Justus, but replied, "Yes." So he packed his clothes. When he went to say good-bye to his friends, many seemed envious. He could not find Justus. The poor fellow simply couldn't bear to see his favorite buddy leave, so he had run away and hid.

Duncan's stomach felt tied in knots as he boarded the *matatu*. *Will my new home be good or bad?* he wondered. Mama Dolphine had spoken of her husband and children. *Will they be as gentle as her? How can I go without Justus?* Mama Dolphine smiled reassuringly and patted his hand as he sat down on the seat beside her clutching his bundle. He tried to return her smile, but with his heart in his throat his smile felt strained.

They got off the bus at the station in Lela. Duncan gazed about wide-eyed, for he had never traveled outside of Kisumu in all of his thirteen years. Mama Dolphine pointed out her *duka* to him before they began walking deep into the interior, far off the main road. As they walked towards the *dala*, she took his hand, and Duncan felt better. With the love of Mama Dolphine, he could face anything.

Just as the evening shadows began to fall, they finally entered the *dala*. Seeing only one grass-thatched, mud hut besides the cookhouse, Duncan knew there was only one wife in this home. Yet when they walked through the door, Duncan's fears materialized into the shape of an old, menacing man who scowled at them from his seat in the dusky hut.

"This is my husband. Just call him Jaduong," Mama Dolphine whispered.

Duncan nodded and on trembling feet made his way to Jaduong. He stretched out his thin hand, and the hard, calloused one shook it roughly.

"You have come," the old man acknowledged. "You will receive your food and clothes in return for your services as a cowherd and field worker." Duncan swallowed and nodded. Mama Dolphine had mentioned none of this to him, but her expression revealed that she was as surprised as he. *I should've known better than to think Jaduong would honor me as a visitor. So now, since I stay here, it is good if I know how to work*, Duncan decided. Just then he thought of something.

"What about school? Will I be attending school?" he asked eagerly. An education was as important to him as any African, even if he found learning difficult. He was sure Mama Dolphine would let him go. But Jaduong had heard Duncan's question.

"You are only an orphan," he scowled. "I do not want to hear any more words about school. It is enough to struggle to find school fees for my real son." Clearly he was unwanted by Jaduong. Before his eyes could fill with tears, Mama Dolphine motioned him to follow her out of the hut where Jaduong could not hear. Her troubled face showed she was disappointed too.

"Duncan," she said soberly, looking into his eyes. "I made a mistake by marrying Jaduong. He is twenty years older than I am and very cruel. I did not tell you about him before because I was afraid you wouldn't want to come with me. Don't be afraid of him. Remember the good part. You are no longer an orphan. You are my son."

Duncan murmured, "*Eee.*" (yes)

"I had thought we would put you through school and give you all the privileges we gave our other children. But it seems you and I are disappointed. I told my husband you would be coming, and he accepted my decision without many words. But only now is when I'm seeing how he feels. Keep this in mind: I am sorry for the way Jaduong acts, but I'm not taking his side. No matter what he says, no matter what he does, I still love you. I will treat you like my other children." The tensions of the day seemed to fade away as Duncan smiled up as his new mother. At long last, he belonged. He might never be accepted by Jaduong, but at least Mama Dolphine loved him.

That night his new mother outdid herself in cooking an extra special meal. She killed a chicken to celebrate and cooked rice and *ugali*. Not only that, but there was tea and bread. Duncan ate to his satisfaction. Mama Dolphine's son Pius ate with them, but he seemed quiet and shy. After supper, Duncan was sent into the cookhouse to sleep with his new brother, who was just a little younger than him.

After a while their tongues loosened up, and Duncan decided Pius wasn't shy after all. His foster brother peppered him with questions about his life before he came to their *dala*. Duncan wasn't sure whether his new brother resented his intrusion into their lives or not. Time would tell.

chapter four
To Build a House

THE WEEKS FADED INTO MONTHS AS DUNCAN MASTERED HIS NEW responsibilities in the home of Mama Dolphine. His new brother, Pius, had shown him where to take Jaduong's cattle every day. Sometimes Duncan and Pius weeded the garden together in the blazing Kenyan sun.

"This is hard work!" Duncan exclaimed as the sweat beaded on his face. It was no small task to stay ahead of the weeds during the rainy season.

"But you, you're not used to it," the younger boy replied. "Wait, and one day you will be strong like me." He proudly flexed his thin brown arm until a little bump stood up. Duncan grinned at his foster brother's boasting. He had become as close to Pius as to Mama Dolphine.

Because Duncan realized he was only an orphan, he tried not to resent his brother for being able to go to school while he had to stay home and work. Most of the time the two brothers got along well.

When Pius went off to school, Duncan harvested the maize alone, although Jaduong helped to shell it off the cobs. The long hours of work made the orphan tall and strong. *Eee, I'll soon be old enough to build my own house!* The thought struck with with a jolt of excitement. Then he sobered. *Maybe Jaduong won't give me the money I need.*

His step-father had remained surly and unresponsive to Duncan's attempts to establish a friendship. The attitude "You are not my real son!" oozed from his every word and action.

Early one morning, Mama Dolphine called Duncan aside and asked him to run an errand for her. "You have stayed with us for over a year now, and you have been a trustworthy person. I need fruits and vegetables from Kisumu market for my roadside shop. Will you go buy them for me?"

Duncan nodded solemnly. "Thanks for trusting me with this job," he replied. When she gave him the money, he trotted off with the empty baskets to the bus stop. *Was it only a year ago I walked this path with Mama Dolphine? I was still young and so afraid,* he pondered.

Duncan enjoyed his day in Kisumu. He purchased the produce without any problem, then decided to look up some of his old friends at the orphanage. When he arrived, he was disappointed to find an empty, run down building. *Maybe the orphanage is not running anymore,* he told himself. Later someone confirmed his suspicions. Mama June had apparently lost valuable support from foreign donors, which forced her to leave her work of charity.

As Duncan walked toward the bus station, it seemed like a dream that he had ever lived on the streets like all the ragged urchins around him. His heart went out to the beggars, and he bought a bunch of bananas to pass out to them.

When he returned to his home in Lela, Jaduong sent him to herd the animals again. "When the sun goes down," he growled, "bring the cattle back here, then go out and cut down the maize stalks where we harvested." Duncan nodded respectfully, then went to relieve his brother, who had been watching the animals in his absence. He would be very tired when the day was over.

"Duncan," Mama Dolphine's voice stopped him. "Thank you for buying the food for my duka." She smiled. "This will be your job every Tuesday."

So the days and months passed, filled with work and activity. Sometimes Duncan smarted with the unfairness of Jaduong's obvious preference for Pius. He allowed his own son to go to school while Duncan had to stay home and work.

But Mama Dolphine would comfort him with her motherly love. "Don't mind Jaduong," she told him. "He is old and bitter because of the trials life has brought him. There is no love in his heart for anyone. Even if he does not love you, I do. Sometimes I think I love you more than my own children."

Duncan was speechless. He knew he did not deserve her affection. What a remarkable woman she was! *Maybe it is because of her religion,* he told himself. *Always, she has been so filled with love. She says God is love. But I know this God is not my God--at least not now. I am still young and I will live long. I don't need God yet.*

One night several years later, Duncan and Pius were lying on their reed mat. Their conversation drifted to Duncan's dream of building a house.

"You are old enough to have your own house," Pius told him.

Duncan nodded enthusiastically, forgetting his brother couldn't see him in the dark. "Does that mean I am also old enough to find a woman to keep it for me?" he asked mischievously.

Pius tried to stifle his laughter. "Of course! Just wait another five years until you are twenty-five or thirty. But how will you find money to build a house?"

Duncan pondered a bit, then replied. "Jaduong would never give me money. Yet if I am to start a business, I need capital. Maybe I will buy a bicycle and do taxi work to earn the money."

"But how will you get money for a bike?" asked Pius. Maybe Jaduong will give me money, but he will not give you any." Pius' words, though matter-of-fact, still stung.

"I can just ask for a loan. If he refuses, I must find a bike some other way." Duncan sighed. "Yet if I build a house, it will not be for quite some time. Money takes time to earn." The conversation drifted to other subjects before sleep claimed the two boys.

Two full weeks passed before Duncan found the courage and a good opportunity to approach Jaduong. The old man's belly was full of *ugali* and cabbage, and he seemed to be in an exceptionally good frame of mind

With fearful trembling, Duncan looked up from his plate and asked, "Jaduong, I have reached the proper age, and want to build my own house."

His foster dad shrugged. He did not care; it was none of his affair.

Duncan wanted to shake him, but went on calmly,

"I need money, but I am not begging you. I am hoping to start a business as a bike taxi. If you can loan me the money for a bike, I would pay back the money as I can. Then I would save for a house. Do you agree to give me a loan?" Duncan's breath came short and fast. Would his foster dad agree?

Jaduong snorted. His yellowish eyes blazed. "You, are you begging me money? I am not your father! Remember, you are only an orphan. You have no right to request me things. If I loan you money for a bike, how do I know you will pay it back? No, just go away. I have no money for a glue-sniffing orphan like you."

Duncan walked away quickly before he would say something he'd regret. He fumed to himself, *Many years I have been working for him like a slave with no pay. But now when I ask for a loan, he insults me by reminding me of my former life! Heh! Mama Dolphine's God does not live in him. Maybe that God is not around at all.*

Mama had not heard her husband's angry words. Duncan was not in the mood for her comfort or endearing words anyway. He fled to the cornfield in a huff. When Pius found him there later, Duncan's eyes were still flaming with rage. He spat out the story to his brother. "I'm very sorry," Pius said sympathetically.

"He did me wrong!" Duncan exploded. "Why should I herd his skinny cows? And I don't need to hoe for him his maize anymore! I am going to work for myself now, although I don't know how I can get a bike." His shoulders slumped in sudden defeat.

Pius' eyes glinted with cunning. "Maybe I could help you find one. I have my ways."

Duncan swung around. "What are you saying? Will you steal one for me?" Relief tinged his voice. Would his foster brother actually do more for him than Jadoung would?

"I will need your help," Pius replied, his voice hard. "Meet me in Ahero by 9:00 next Tuesday morning."

"Okay," Duncan replied. "I'll be there."

chapter five

Hard Work for a House

True to his word, Pius waited for Duncan in the deserted alleyway in Ahero. Duncan's eyes popped when he saw the Japanese-made bicycle propped against the building.

"How did you get that? Did . . . did you . . .?" Duncan stammered.

Pius waved airily toward the bike. "I have . . . um . . . er, gotten this bicycle for you," he explained. "Soon you can begin your bike taxi service. Then you will find money for your house. If you have enough shillings for a small can of paint, hadn't we better get to work?"

"Why?" asked Duncan stupidly.

Pius sighed in exasperation. "Must I explain every detail to you? We need to change the look of this bike. You wouldn't want the former owner... well... getting it back."

"Oh," Duncan replied. Something told him he should not accept the bicycle, since Pius had stolen it. He chose to ignore his conscience; however, and bought a small can of paint and few brushes from a nearby shop. The two brothers set about to change the bike's appearance.

While they painted, Duncan badgered Pius until he described how he had acquired the bike. "I was with my friends last night in Kisumu, and we were walking down a back street. As we went along, we saw two white boys riding their bikes. Before they saw us, we surprised them by jumping on them and beating them. The two boys fought with us, but I pulled the newer bike away. So here is the bike; it is yours."

Duncan nodded his thanks. So it was stolen property. What else could he do but accept it? He did need the bike! He rode home with guilty pleasure. *I didn't steal it, really, but I accepted stolen property from Pius*, he worried. *That was wrong. What am I going to tell Mama Dolphine? I'll have to lie and cover up. Of course, I've done this before--we street boys lied and stole every day.*

When Mama saw Pius and Duncan ride in, she exclaimed in surprise, "Where did you find such a nice bicycle? How did you get the money?" She rubbed the smooth fender and eyed the neat passenger seat over the back wheel that Pius had helped Duncan buy. "Duncan, will you begin bike taxi work?"

Duncan held up his hand. "Ask me only one question at a time!" he said with a forced chuckle.

"Okay," Mama Dolphine replied. " How did you get this bike?" She admired the lovely shine of its new paint.

"Mama, I have a *misungu* (white) friend who is a pastor in the Anglican church. I told him how I need a job, so he lent me the money, which I will pay back slowly as I earn wage." The rehearsed story rolled off his tongue as glibly as in the old days.

Mama Dolphine's eyebrows rose. "Why have I never heard of this *misungu* pastor before? Are you telling me the truth?" Duncan nodded, looking her in the eye.

In the following days, his mother tried to obtain proof of how he had gotten the bicycle, but found no evidence against him. After a few days, she threw up her hands, and said, "I don't know if you were really given such a large loan. If you stole it, God knows. "

"I did not steal it. I got the bike in a good way," Duncan insisted, putting on a poker face. Mama Dolphine just shrugged. So Duncan began his work of transporting people and hauling freight whenever he could find someone who needed a bike taxi.

For several years, Duncan saved money to begin buying materials for his first house. Like many bike-taxi drivers, he became entangled in immorality. The more conviction he felt because of his fornication, the more he indulged in short-lived pleasure to cover up his gnawing misery.

Yet things were going quite well financially. He had already stored most of the large sisal poles under the overhang of Jaduong's roof and was working on earning shillings for *fetos*. (thin wooden poles) For his first house, he would use a grass thatch. Later when he could afford to build another house outside his father's *dala*, he would use tin for the roof so it would last longer.

After another year when the *fetos* had joined the larger poles in the storage place, Pius asked Duncan, "Are you knowing about the abandoned sugar cane fields where grass may be slashed freely?"

"No--where?"

"Somewhere close to Kajulu."

"That is too far to haul grass with a bicycle."

Pius joked, "But maybe the white pastor who gave you a bike will haul the grass for you on his vehicle." Seeing Duncan's raised eyebrows, he laughed. "You know I am just 'playing' about him giving you the bike. But there is a white missionary pastor who may agree to help you. Mama Dolphine and I have been attending his church. She is going for different reasons than I, of course." He winked wickedly. "My friendship with him can benefit us, see? I will ask him to help us."

"Good!" cheered Duncan. "I will go slash that grass. Will you help me? I'll pay you fifty shillings a day." Pius agreed, and so they traveled in a matatu to the field of grass the next morning. They cut the grass with a curved tool called a slasher. Tying grass into bundles and swinging the slashers made the sweat bead on their foreheads.

"Pius, did you bring anything to drink?"

His foster brother looked surprised. "I didn't think to bring water or even a little *nyuka*. But I think we'll do all right without it."

Duncan nodded, unconcerned. He was used to a forced fast now and then. By evening, when Duncan was so tired he felt he could not swing his slasher one more stroke, he told Pius, "It is time to go home! Let's store the bundles of grass in that hut which seems vacant." Indeed, the walls were crumbling, and the thatch missing in many places. Once they were satisfied no thieves would find their grass, the two brothers waited at the road for a matatu and rode to Lela.

After they arrived at the *dala*, the hungry young men gobbled mounds of Mama Dolphine's fresh *ugali* with *sakumu*. (fried collard greens) Following a quick bath, they both collapsed on their reed mat and immediately fell into an exhausted sleep.

The next day, they returned to slash more grass. Once Duncan decided they had enough cut, they rested in the shade until the white pastor arrived. He kindly stacked all their bundles of grass on his Cruiser's roof rack. Duncan thanked him for helping and promised to attend his church. *Of course I will not really go to the church. I am just being polite*, he reasoned.

Now that the grass was safely at Lela, Duncan was finally ready to begin building! With exhilaration, he approached his stepfather about a possible site for his house. Respectfully, Duncan said, "Jadoung, I have collected my own materials to begin building my house. Where would be the best spot to build it?"

The old man scowled from under his shaggy white eyebrows. "Why ask me? My land belongs only to my own sons! You know very well you are only an orphan and once a glue sniffer. Go buy land somewhere else." Then he turned his back to indicate the conversation was over.

Duncan slumped in despair. It seemed everywhere he turned his stepfather opposed him. *Aaii, he refuses to hear a word! If I try to explain things to him, it will only become worse. There is nothing to do but plead with Mama Dolphine.*

By this time, Mama was regularly attending the white man's church in Ahero. She had always been loving and kind, but now she seemed to have a new peace. As far as Duncan knew, she was not receiving any financial help because she always had plenty of money. Jaduong had much land and cattle, and Mama Dolphine had her *duka*. Duncan and Mama Dolphine were still close, although he knew Mama didn't approve of his lifestyle on the job.

"Mama Dolphine," he began hesitantly.

She looked up from chopping vegetables and smiled. *"Eee?"*

"I have stored all the materials I need to build my house. However, Jadoung told me his land is only for his own sons."

Mama's eyes spat fire, but she only said, "I will speak to him about this matter."

Duncan never heard their conversation. He often wondered how Mama had persuaded Jadoung to give in, but one morning the old man hobbled up to Duncan on his cane. "You may build your house there." One gnarled finger pointed to the site.

Duncan's mouth dropped open. "Thank you, Jaduong," he replied, trying to conceal his surprise. Mama Dolphine's words and prayers must have been effective! His stepfather only grunted and returned to his chair under the shade tree.

A little rain fell the morning of the house raising, but Duncan's friends started trickling in by 10:00. The drizzle soon disappeared. Some of Mama Dolphine's church friends came too, so Duncan asked the American pastor to bless the ground. According to Luo culture, he must pray before any work could be done on the little plot of land. This should take care of any spirits lingering on the site.

In obedience to Luo tradition, Duncan had to carry a rooster, an axe, and some hot coals of fire to the building site. He wasn't sure why, but he had been told if he did not follow the dictates of their culture, he might get thin and die. *Maybe there's a Luo custom I don't know. Maybe I'm disobeying a rule, and I might still die of the curse of chira!* Duncan worried.

Raising his hands to the sky, Pastor William prayed, "Father in Heaven, thank You for giving us this new day. As this house is built, bless all who work. Keep harm from us. Bless Duncan as he lives there. Bless this ground where the house is built. In Jesus' Name," All joined in on the "Amen."

Most of Jaduong's clan had come, as custom demanded. The clan elders who were too old to work rested in the shade and visited together. Mama Dolphine and a few of Jaduong's neighboring relatives cooked *nyoyo* (corn cooked with beans) and *nyuka* next to a reed mat set up on end to provide shade.

The men, wielding their sharp digging irons, began to dig holes for the four posts of the hut's corners. Duncan and Pius plowed the ground nearby with oxen. Water would be poured on the loose soil for mudding the house. The carpenter in charge helped nail together the rafters, and everyone watched as they put up the hut's framework and nailed it in place. Duncan had decided to use sisal strips to tie the *fetos* on, since this was much cheaper than nails. The women began carrying water from the river to pour on the plowed ground to make mud. Some of the men turned up their pant legs so as to be able to work the mud with their feet like a giant mixer.

The roof was partially spread with grass. Now Duncan's cousins and aunts and some white-veiled ladies from Mama Dolphine's church began to cram globs of thick, gooey mud between the poles and *fetos*. Before nightfall, all the walls were filled in with mud. Mama Dolphine and some of her helpers had served chai with *nyoyo* at lunch. After all the work was done, they fed everyone a wonderful meal of *ugali* and duck.

Duncan sighed with relief. "I didn't know if we'd finish today. The women didn't come until afternoon, and they were few. A house must be finished the same day it's built," he told Pius.

His brother nodded seriously. "We cannot allow the spirits to sleep inside the first night. Even me, I am soon to build, since I am the next oldest son. I would like to become a carpenter, but I have no money to buy tools. Therefore, I am planning to apprentice in a coffin shop in a week. The carpenter can teach me the trade while I earn money for my business."

Duncan clapped him on the back. "That is good! Building a house takes a lot of hard work and time, but as you can see, it's possible. And it's more special since I earned the money myself."

"Never forget the one who brought the bike for you. That is how it began," Pius reminded him with a grin. Duncan nodded, but hung his head. *Why did I ever accept the bike? It makes me feel so guilty,* he sighed to himself. Silently, he moved his few possessions into the damp, new house.

As he lay down to sleep, his mind returned to the events of the day. Those Christians from his mother's church--the women in their white veils, the men with their godly ways--had made a deep impression on him. He wished for the peace they radiated. But alas, he was too deeply involved in his immoral ways. Could he ever find an escape from the guilt and misery?

chapter six

A New Church

DUNCAN STRETCHED AS HE AWOKE IN HIS NEW HOUSE. *IT IS A NICE morning*, he sighed contentedly. After getting dressed, he joined Pius and Jaduong for breakfast in Mama Dolphine's house.

They sipped their morning chai as Jaduong' announced shortly, "Today we harvest maize." Duncan and Pius stifled a collective groan at their father's words. Duncan remembered seeing the maize stalks, heavy with plump ears. The brown husks showed the maize was nicely dried, since the season of long rains had tapered off. Thinking of the hard work ahead of them, the brothers soberly drank another cup of chai. Duncan grabbed a pile of gunny sacks from the kitchen hut to put the maize into, and they headed for the field.

Beginning at one end of the field, they husked the maize on the stalks and threw the cobs onto piles. They bent each stalk, as they picked the ears, in order to mark which ones were harvested. The rains had been plentiful this year, so the crop was more productive than usual.

"Aaaiiii!" Duncan exclaimed over a huge cob with plump kernels. "I've not yet seen maize so nice as this. Actually, harvesting today is better than last harvest when we picked those little nubbins."

Pius only nodded, his shaved head gleaming cheerfully in the sun's morning rays. After an hour or two, Duncan moaned, "I feel hot, itchy, and thirsty."

"Even me," said Pius. "But we still have a lot of work, even with Mama Dolphine putting the cobs in gunny sacks for us. You ought to be glad I'm not in school like the other children. I don't stay home every day to help with harvest."

Duncan nodded. "I'm glad for your help. Even me, I long to go further in school than standard four. I know how to do sums, and I can read in Luo, but I don't speak English very well."

Mama Dolphine looked up from bagging maize. "Many young men your age still go to school, Duncan," she said. "However, I think those days are over for you because Jaduong will not agree to pay your fees." She stopped to deposit a pile of maize in her sack. "Why don't you try to gain some education in my church? The entire service is translated into Luo, and you could learn some English. Besides, the Word of God will give you peace." Mama walked over to the next pile of cobs.

How does she know I want peace? I have never talked to her about the heaviness I've been carrying, Duncan pondered. *But I'm not ready to become a good man yet. If I go to the white man's church, it will be to learn English, not hear the Word of God.*

"Maybe I'll come; maybe not," he hedged to Mama Dolphine. She wisely refrained from pressing him.

The next Sunday morning he came to join the others, dressed in his best clothes. Duncan watched Pius' eyebrows shoot up.

"Aaaiiii! Are you coming to church with us?"

Duncan nodded. "I'm going to the white man's house of worship to learn English," he explained.

His brother tried to keep a straight face. "I think you are just wanting to see how they worship."

"I'm going to learn English," Duncan maintained, then added, "I'm not going to worship, even as you also are not going to worship. But I'm not going with the hidden agenda of getting money like you are."

It was Pius' turn to get angry. "Maybe I told you some Americans are generous and do things like hauling grass. And maybe I get a gift now and then. But me, I'm not a beggar, you glue sniffer!"

Never before had Pius flung Duncan's past into his face like this. Duncan had always enjoyed the acceptance and friendship of his adopted younger brother. Pius' cruel words stung, but Duncan tried to brush them off. He strode down the path with his foster brother. Mama Dolphine soon joined them, puffing from her little jog to catch up.

"Oh Duncan, I'm so glad you are going with us," she exclaimed when she had caught her breath. Duncan only nodded. He was not in the mood to do any elaborating. They walked the long path out to Onjiko where the church was located.

Soon they entered the stone building where many other Kenyans were singing Luo songs. Duncan didn't know the words, having rarely been to church. But he had heard them sung at numerous funerals, so the tunes were vaguely familiar.

The devotional was led by an old man with a deep, mellow voice. When Duncan heard him teaching against things like lying, stealing, and fornication, he squirmed on the bench. Ping! He noticed the tall man beside him had a tap-bell. As soon as the old man by the pulpit heard the bell, he quickly wound up his topic and led in prayer. Duncan breathed a sigh of relief.

The tall man beside him unwound his long legs and strode to the front. He asked the children to go to the back rooms. Duncan was puzzled. Then a very black man went to the pulpit with his interpreter and began to teach a Bible lesson. He read a Scripture, and anyone was invited ask questions or give answers. As Duncan became engrossed in the discussion, soon he forgot all about learning English. But he felt more and more uncomfortable as he realized that he was doing many wrong things in his life. *I'm a sinner*, he thought with a start. *I have displeased God and deserve punishment!*

Duncan bent over and buried his face in his hands. *Do I want Jesus to change my life?* he agonized. *Can I leave my immoral living? I don't think so.* Duncan sat back up.

After a while, the man with the bell jerked around to look at the clock. With an astonished start, he pinged the bell sharply three times. Soon children came pouring out of both rooms. The younger set stood up front and tried to recite a verse, but they did rather poorly in keeping together. They did sing very sweetly. Some of the older children took turns reciting their verse alone, but Duncan didn't understand it since they spoke in English.

Soon Pastor William went to the pulpit and asked for prayer requests. It seemed nearly everybody was either sick or had a sick relative. One young man asked for prayer so that he might become a stronger Christian. Duncan was secretly impressed. After pastor William had prayed for them, he led the congregation in a song.

For the first time, Duncan noticed two little *wasungu* boys on the front bench. They're probably Pastor William's sons, he thought. Duncan noticed they did a lot of whispering and passing notes with the Luo boys sitting with them.

During the pastor's sermon about the prodical son, Duncan was so convicted he nearly walked out, remaining in his seat only because he feared appearing conspicuous. His stomach churned with turmoil. "There is joy in heaven over one sinner who repents!" the pastor exclaimed. "Even the worst sinner can come to God."

This white man doesn't know me. He has no idea anyone can be such a sinner as me, Duncan reasoned. His head went down on his knees again.

"Only believe in Jesus, and you will be saved. If you accept him as your Saviour, and allow His blood to cleanse your sin, you will be clean before God. After that He will give you grace to leave your wicked ways. You must leave wrong cultural practices." Duncan's head jerked up. *What does this mean?*

The pastor continued, "Leave things like wife inheritance, polygamy, and superstitions like going to the witch doctor." Duncan quivered slightly. He wished with all his heart this service would soon be over.

Finally the service was closed, and everyone knelt for prayer. Duncan was unaccustomed to kneeling. But in order not to be rude, he complied. After prayer, many people wanted to testify. Some old mamas wanted to tell long stories of things which had happened to them. Others wanted to confess sin or say "Amen" to the message.

The pastor said, "If anyone wants special prayer for salvation, wait for me in the back room, and I'll pray with you. Sisters can go to the room to my right, and my wife will pray with you." Mama Dolphine eyed Duncan meaningfully. His shoulders slumped. *I love her so much and don't want to displease her,* he thought. *But I can't do this thing until I'm sure! I won't do it just to please her.* They walked to the bus stop mostly in silence. Duncan felt Mama's keen displeasure with him. He had failed to respond for salvation according to her wish. But he didn't feel ready. His sins bound him too tightly. After the taxi ride, they trecked back to their dala. Mama Dolphine finally asked him, "Duncan, how did you like the service?"

Without looking her in the eye, he replied, "It was very good. The pastor has trained his members well."

Mama threw up her chubby hands with frustration. "An answer like that I don't want. I want to know--did you like what the pastor had to say?" "Yes," Duncan lied. He wished to change the subject somehow; this was leading nowhere good. "I attended to learn English, but I found this is not a good place to learn. The interpreter talked too fast, so I couldn't understand him."

"Oh," she said with disappointment. "So you won't be coming back?"

"I'll come back," he reassured Mama Dolphine insincerely, just to satisfy her.

Pius' eyes twinkled, but he held his peace. Duncan wondered how he managed to make it through every service without feeling guilty, since Pius' life was every bit as sinful as his own. When they reached home, he ate *ugali* and *sakumu* with Pius and Jaduong while Mama Dolphine ate in the cookhouse. "So you are afraid of learning English in the white man's church?" Pius mocked. Duncan badly wanted to get back onto good terms with his brother. He decided to be honest. "No, it is not like that. I didn't like the way they preached," he admitted. "How do you manage to keep on attending? You sit there like a hypocrite. Don't the pastor's words convict you?"

No," Pius replied quickly. "I like sitting in church and making the pastor think I'm saved. If I cheat the pastor like that, that shows I'm smart, right? And then I can benefit materially. The white people are very generous." Duncan was shocked. "How can you just sit there and pretend? Doesn't the preaching make you want to run away?" He scooped up some sakuma with his wad of *ugali*.

"I don't want to be saved." Pius replied with his mouth full. "I don't care what the pastor says. I still want to have some fun. After a while, the word of God does not move me. I can sit there and think of other things." He laughed shamelessly.

All this time Jaduong had been silent, although this was not unusual. None of the old man's words were wasted. But now he spoke unexpectedly, treating Pius and Duncan to a sight of partially chewed green and yellow food. "If you boys go to church, you should go for the right reasons. Pius, quit going to church until the day you go as a truthful person. Duncan, stop pretending to learn English. All of you, stay at home." *It seems Jaduong can be wise when he wants to be,* Duncan mused.

chapter seven
Marriage

ONE DAY THE NEXT WEEK, DUNCAN BIKED OUT TO AHERO AS USUAL TO wait for taxi customers. He was soon rattling down the dusty footpath with a slender young lady on his back seat, holding a heavy sack of maize. Duncan had discovered being friendly gave him added job security. Because of this, his customers often returned to him when they needed a lift.

He struck up a conversation with the lady on the back of his bike. "My names are Duncan Odhiambo. I am coming from Lela. What are your names?"

Her little-girl voice softly answered, "I am called Alseba Akinyi. I live in Boya."

"What will you do with this sack of maize?" he asked her curiously.

She replied, "I buy this maize from the mountains to sell in Boya. I need to help support my mother and siblings. My father is mentally unbalanced from smoking opium. Nowadays he walks about as a madman." Duncan accepted the information as though this were nothing out of the ordinary, for there were many such people roaming about in Kenya.

When he had dropped her off, he waited at the nearest bike taxi hangout for his next customer. After Duncan had waited idly for several hours, the same young lady reappeared.

"I want to go back to Ahero for more maize," she told him, springing onto his seat. Duncan found her very easy to converse with as they flew along the path, and after several weeks of hauling maize for her, they became friends.

In the weeks that followed, Duncan met Alseba often as he commuted to and fro. Whenever he talked to Alseba, time seemed to stand still. He recounted his early life on the streets, the time he spent at the orphanage, and his good life with Mama Dolphine. "I guess I'm just lucky!" he told her. "But Jaduong does not claim me as his son. He has always been harsh to me."

"Oh, I'm sorry," she sympathized. "Do they have any other children?"

"I think there are a few daughters who have gone to cook in other places. But there is one son named Pius remaining at home. He is a good brother to me."

As the months passed, Duncan realized he loved Alseba very deeply. *Even though she is not perfect, she is the most wonderful person I've ever met,* he thought.

Months passed. One evening as Duncan and Pius shared their evening meal of *ugali* around Mama Dolphine's fire, Duncan told Pius about his girlfriend. "Alseba is a tiny lady, beautiful, and strong. She's also a fine business woman who knows how to work. We love talking together. I didn't mean to call attention to myself, but the other bike taxi drivers laugh at me because our discussions get so long! She is my best friend."

"So if you love her, why not bring her to live with you? Are you going to take dowry for her?" Pius asked.

Duncan winced. "You know as well as I do there is no money for dowry. And there's no use asking Jaduong for a cow or two. He would not agree. Are you having any good plans to get money quickly?"

Pius shook his head. "I don't have. Are you in a hurry to get married?" he asked.

"Yes," Duncan replied. "She is with child. She is planning to move in with me next week since I cannot pay cows. I will pay the bride price and dowry later, and then we will be married according to Kenyan law. You know everybody is doing like that." His words were bold, but inside he squirmed uncomfortably.

"No problem," Pius reassured him. "Nowadays it is a hard thing to find enough money to do things in a good way. I'm seeing it as okay, even if Mama Dolphine will not accept. In the white man's church she goes to, they require couples to be married in a church and get a certificate."

Duncan sighed. "That takes money, right?" Pius shrugged. Duncan went on, "Even if Pastor William would do the ceremony for free, will he agree if I do not go to his church? Besides, I'd have to wait for three weeks so that we could be published the required length of time. I can't wait that long!"

Pius advised him, "Do what you need to do. I think you've waited long enough for a wife. If you've found the one you want, take her."

"Yes, I will take her," Duncan decided, shoving his guilt aside.

The next week, Duncan transported Alseba and her suitcase to his home in Lela with no fuss or ceremony. According to the custom of the day, they were married. *Or are we really married?* This nagging thought continued to bother Duncan.

Mama Dolphines' reaction didn't make him feel any better. When she returned from buying fruits and vegetables at Kisumu market, she found a small lady in Duncan's house.

Alseba shyly approached her mother-in-law with a courteous handshake. Duncan had warned her that it would take time for Mama Dolphine to warm up to her. "I am Alseba, Duncan's wife. How are you?" she murmured in her little-girl voice.

"Fine," Mama said stiffly, looking Duncan's wife over from head to toe. "So you are here." Her appraisal was not much different than Jaduong's when Duncan had entered this dala for the first time. Disapproval seeped from every pore of Mama Dolphine's body. She waddled back to her own house with not another word.

When Duncan returned from his job that evening, his mother was waiting for him. "What have you done?" she huffed.

"I have married a wife," he replied, trying to look nonchalant. *I knew she would disapprove*, he tried to tell himself.

"This is what you call marriage?" Mama asked, her voice rising louder.

"Shhh!" Duncan put his finger on her lips. "You don't want Alseba to hear you." Mama brushed his finger aside while Duncan went on, "I have married. Even if it is not according to old Luo culture, nowadays it is acceptable. Surely you know I could not afford dowry."

"But you found money in some way for a house," she reminded him with forced gentleness.

"I worked for my house. But it would take too long to save up for cows. You can see Alseba will give birth before too many months. We want to get married now." Duncan set his chin stubbornly.

"This is sin! I have taught you this is wrong! How can you go against my teaching?" Mama Dolphine's voice was full of anguish.

Duncan shrugged and walked away.

chapter eight

A Lust for Wealth

Tɪᴍᴇ sᴘᴇᴅ ʙʏ ғᴏʀ Dᴜɴᴄᴀɴ ᴀɴᴅ Aʟsᴇʙᴀ ᴀs ʟɪғᴇ ғᴇʟʟ ɪɴᴛᴏ ᴀ ᴘʟᴇᴀsᴀɴᴛ routine. By and by, Mama Dolphine came to accept Alseba as one of her daughters. To Duncan's surprise, the two women actually became close friends. They often went to Kisumu market together or chatted as Mama taught Alseba how Duncan liked his food cooked. One day he overheard them in the cookhouse as he was fixing his bike chain outside.

"Use cilantro for flavoring with the tomatoes and onions." Duncan imagined Mama Dolphine showing Alseba how to cut up the lacy herb resembling carrot leaves.

"Umm, smells so good!" Alseba sounded pleased. "You bought this at market?"

"*Eee,*" Mama answered. "Duncan used to carry my basket for me every Tuesday at Jubilee Market." The tantalizing aroma of ripe *ugali* teased Duncan's nostrils.

Alseba giggled. "Duncan already told me all about how you befriended him during the time he stayed at an orphanage. But I'd like to hear your side of the story too."

Duncan finally got the bike chain back on, but he wanted to hear more of their conversation. Just then Mama poked her head out the door and caught him eavesdropping.

"I see you!" she remonstrated.

"But I'm just fixing my bike." Duncan defended himself with an expression of wounded innocence. Then he grinned. "It was interesting to hear you, though. Seems you like my wife after all."

Mama pretended to swat him away. "I don't think you made a bad choice, but I still wish you would have married her in God's way. Now, since I decided to make the best of it, I've discovered Alseba is a really nice lady."

"Of course, I chose a wonderful girl!" Duncan was triumphant. "Would you have expected anything less of me?"

"Conceited, are you?" she teased. "Yes, I trained you to look for a good wife. I'm pleased with the character of your lady. But be sure your sins will find you out. I call it fornication, not marriage."

Duncan shuffled over his house guiltily, waiting for the women to bring in his lunch. *There wasn't any other choice,* he tried to excuse himself. But he couldn't shake Mama's convicting words from his mind.

Alseba gave birth to a son, much to Duncan's delight. "We'll name him Otieno," Alseba told her husband, looking lovingly into their son's puffy, round face. They knew his light skin would change into the swarthy black of the Luo after several weeks.

"Yes, he was born at night, so Otieno he shall be," Duncan replied. Duncan and Alseba loved their new son, but it meant Duncan had to work harder. Alseba asked him for money to buy baby-care products, but she had to make do with the bare essentials because his job paid so little. Many months passed, and Otieno grew rapidly.

"I wish there weren't so many bike-taxi drivers," Duncan agonized to Alseba one evening. Otieno, who was old enough to sit alone now, amused himself on the floor with a flip-flop. "With more drivers, there is not as much demand. My regular customers still give me business, but this job just doesn't make enough money!"

Alseba picked up the fussing baby and started nursing him. "You probably heard Pius got a job with the white pastor, Mr. William, now that he is baptized. Do you think he makes more than you?"

"I don't know," Duncan replied with a sigh. "I know he only works one day a week, but that's a good way to supplement his other meager earnings. With the dry season upon us, everyone suffers."

Alseba looked worried. "Yes, our store of maize from last harvest is nearly all gone. We need to wait until the long rains come to plant again, but I don't know if we have enough resources to make it until next harvest."

Duncan shook his head. "That is always difficult. But somehow, we've got to make it. I'll talk to Pius sometime to see if he has any ideas," he encouraged his young wife.

Several weeks later, after Pius had returned from his job for the white pastor, Duncan strolled over to the shade tree to chat. "How was your day?" he inquired casually.

"Just great!" Pius replied. "The work is good and so is the pay. It helps me a lot, especially since I'm saving for a house." He gestured toward the *fetos* and grass he was storing in the cookhouse.

"Yes, I'm glad for you. But what about me? My wife and son will go hungry after our maize is gone, and my taxi work doesn't pay enough. Soon I shall need to find work in someone else's fields."

"Everyone is complaining about hunger these days. I hope the long rains come soon," Pius sympathized. He did not offer to give his brother a handout. But his eyes held a far-away look, and Duncan knew he had a plan cooking.

Suddenly Pius snapped his fingers. "I know what! The missionaries often keep large sums of money in their compound; I know exactly which room. But they usually lock their shillings in a fire safe. Sometimes, however, the safe is left unlocked. If we're lucky, we can find some money free for the taking!"

Duncan hesitated. "But if you are a church member and they hire you to work, what if they find out you are a thief? They might take away your job and church membership. Besides, I'm afraid they'll catch us and jail us!"

"Oh, they'll never find out," Pius assured him. "We are both used to stealing. Why, if they knew what all I've already taken from them, they'd never hire me again! I'm smart enough to cover my tracks," he bragged.

"Okay," Duncan agreed reluctantly. "This may be my only way of getting the money I need. Besides food, Alseba needs a cookhouse badly, and I know I'll need a large sum for building materials. Also, we are expecting another little one. Children are such an expense!" He paused and thought about what he'd just said. "But I'm not sorry I got married, and I love my son Otieno", he amended.

"You'll get your money, all right," Pius sounded confident. "Come see me in a week. Meet me after dark at Lela primary school. Don't tell a soul what you're up to. Don't even tell Alseba. Promise?"

Promise," Duncan agreed. He walked back to his little family with mixed feelings of apprehension and excitement. As he drifted to sleep, all he could see in his mind were wads of thousand-shilling bills.

In a week, Duncan met Pius after dark as he had promised. They biked silently down the path to the road, then flagged down a public van on its last journey to Kisumu. Pius grinned and elbowed Duncan, but Duncan hid his butterflies. When they alighted from the van and started walking to the compound, Pius began whispering instructions.

"We must get past the guard at the gate first of all. He knows me, so I don't think he'll worry about letting me in. I'll tell him we need help for a sick relative. Our next hurdle is getting to the house without the dogs being too noisy. Luckily for us, this evening the missionaries are having a prayer service together. It is the bishop's turn to host the meeting, and they live outside the compound. So no one will be around. See the beauty of the plan?"

Duncan gave him a wobbly grin, then asked, "What if the safe is locked?" His eyes darted back and forth. "What if they come home from prayer meeting and catch us?"

"Don't worry!" Pius said. "Luck will be on our side. No one will know. Just remember, this wealth is ours by right. We are poor children of Africa, and these rich Americans should share with us. We will take only what should belong to us!"

Duncan shrugged. By this time they had reached the gate. He noticed Pius saluted the guard, so he followed suit.

"Good evening," Pius greeted the guard. "I need to see the pastor because my mother is very sick. He must take her to the hospital. She might not last till morning. My brother has accompanied me."

The guard waved them both through the gate. "Come in and wait for the pastor," he urged them. "He has gone for a meeting, but he will be back soon. I'm sorry to hear of your sick mother."

"God will help her," Duncan piped up in the customary manner of the Luo. He followed Pius to one of the identical houses. Thankfully, the dogs knew Pius and made no commotion.

"The best way into these houses is through the roof," Pius whispered. "We will be undetected since we are not breaking in through a window or a door." He motioned for Duncan to follow, then climbed onto the roof, and began removing roofing tiles. Each small noise seemed amplified in the still of the night. Once a tile gave a loud clank and both men froze in terror. They listened for the dogs, but heard no barking. The thieves continued their work swiftly and silently. Then Pius descended into the attic.

His whisper wafted from the dark hole, "You come down, and I'll show you the way to the office. But be careful to step on the beams so you don't fall through a ceiling tile." Gingerly, Duncan followed. His hands shook.

When they were both in the attic, Pius opened a little trapdoor. "I want you to go down through here, and then enter the first door to your right," he instructed. "You will see a little stand covered by a blue cloth. Look under the cloth to see whether the safe is locked. If you can unlatch the little door, search as quickly as possible for money."

Duncan's eyes popped. "But … suppose somebody catches us!"

"Don't worry," Pius assured him. "I am going back up on the roof to stand guard in case anything looks suspicious. The missionaries know me, so if I get off the roof quickly enough, I can explain our presence to them. You'll need to get out of the house, though. But I'll warn you in time."

"Okay," Duncan agreed. "I must be quick when I'm coming back up, though. How do I get up and down?"

"Jump down," Pius replied. "To come back up, put a chair under the trap door and I'll pull you up. Okay, now hurry!"

Pius disappeared onto the roof. There was nothing left for Duncan to do but jump. His heart pounded in his ears. Easing himself through the hole, he let go. *Thud!* It sounded like thunder to him. Along the way, he left dirty footprints. Then he scurried through the door Pius had indicated.

Once inside, his eyes darted to a small stand with a blue cloth. *There!* He lifted the cloth, and his eyes glowed greedily when he saw the little door was unlocked. *Quick! Not much time,* he told himself. Desperately, he rooted through the envelopes of passports and other important documents. Then he found a fat envelope of thousand-shilling bills. He grabbed it.

"Psstt!" Duncan jumped when he heard Pius' warning. He clutched the envelope with a sweaty palm and ran out to the hallway.

"Get up here as fast as you can!" Pius cried in a hoarse whisper. "Grab a chair in the kitchen." Duncan ran and dragged the chair under the hole. Pius helped him up, and soon they were back on the roof.

"Look!" Pius pointed. "She's coming back early from the prayer meeting!"

Duncan looked down on the street to see none other than the pastor's daughter. "We're done for," he moaned with a terrible sinking feeling.

chapter nine

Rumors

DUNCAN AND PIUS SCRAMBLED OFF THE ROOF. HURRIEDLY, THEY SLID down and slunk into the shadows. *Has the pastor's daughter seen us?* Duncan strained his eyes and saw her strolling to the house at the far end of the compound.

"Maybe we'll get away!" Pius whispered. Once she had disappeared into the house, they walked to the main gate as calmly as they could. Duncan's heart pounded and his hands grew clammy as they approached the gate guard.

"The pastor was not around, so we are leaving," Pius explained smoothly as they approached him. The guard was wearing a hooded coat and socks on his hands to ward off the evening chill.

"Okay," the guard replied to Pius' report. Duncan raised his eyebrows. *Why wasn't the watchman asking more questions?* He would ask Pius later.

Pius seemed to read his mind. Once they were on a public vehicle bound for Lela, he whispered slyly, "Were you surprised with the way the guard asked so few questions at the gate?"

"*Eee.* Did you pay him a bribe so that he would be silent?" Duncan questioned.

Pius tried to muffle his laughter in his shirt sleeve. "One thousand shillings only," he replied. "They don't pay this old guard very much for his menial job, so I know he was happy for what I gave him." Pius seemed to think this was a joke.

Duncan brooded. *Yes, we poor Luo stole from the rich white men, but was it really the right thing to do? Paying a bribe was not honest, either. But I can't let that bother me too much. Alseba will be very happy when I build her the new cookhouse that she's been requesting me.* But he couldn't help squirming a little.

After they alighted at Lela and arrived at the dala, Pius split the booty with his foster brother. To Duncan, the thick wads seemed to glow in the dark. *Eee-eh, it feels good to have this much pesa.* (money) He shoved all the guilty thoughts into a vague corner of his mind.

The next week, Duncan built a cute, sturdy cookhouse for his common-law wife. Alseba beamed her thanks as she mudded the walls shut. "But where did you get the money?" she persistently inquired.

He watched her cram another wad of mud between the wooden poles as he racked his mind for a neat story. Finally, he gave up. "Pius helped me find the money. You know what I mean."

Her eyes threw sparks. "Do you think I agree with everything Pius does? Does he need to draw you into his bad plans? If he wanted to steal money, did he have to make you as much a child of hell as he is?"

He winced at her words, but replied, "If Pius is a child of hell, I am also one. But it's true--we must eat, and you need a place to cook. You know our sons also need a place to sleep after they are older, according to our culture. They can sleep in the kitchen."

Alseba nodded meekly. "Eeee. You did well to build me a kitchen. Thanks very much." As was expected of a submissive Luo wife, she said no more.

The next day, Duncan rode his bike to Ahero for his normal bike taxi job. He happened to be transporting a firey-tempered young man to Kobongo when he heard some interesting news.

"Look at this building!" Sampson exclaimed. "This is where the white devil-worshipers meet to suck the blood of Luos."

Duncan tried to stifle his gasp. *This is the very church Mama Dolphine is a member of! How can this be true?*

Sampson went on quickly, "Yes they worship demons. They are known to bribe children with candy in order to kidnap them for body parts and blood. They walk into the church with their backs turned, and are pulling people from many other churches to join them. They pull them with money and things."

"Who told you this?" asked Duncan cautiously.

"Why haven't you ever heard this before? All people in town have heard this word. These people have been going on with their terrible deeds since '94!"

"You worship with which church?" Duncan asked.

"Me, I don't go to church. But I am thinking we must do something so these awful people stop doing so much damage in Kenya."

Duncan was silent as the incensed man on the seat behind him fumed about the white man's church. *These are lies*, he decided. *Mama Dolphine is the best Christian I know. She could not go to a Satan-worshipping church.* In fact, he had personally witnessed one of their services and had been impressed, even spiritually convicted.

"Sampson, how do you know this is true?" Duncan asked him. "Have you ever been to this church yourself?"

"Me, I'm not going there. I'm not allowing someone to drink my blood!"

He is foolish, thought Duncan. However, had he never personally witnessed the life of Mama Dolphine and attended her church, he would be tempted to believe the lies himself.

Duncan knew Sampson's words was far-fetched. But without thinking, he retold the story to the next gossipy mama on his bike route. Subconsciously, it was his way of getting back at God for all the guilt he'd felt in his life. He needed a means of revenge for his years of rejection.

That evening, he retold the story to Alseba, being careful to avoid mentioning the name of the church.

"How dreadful!" Her big, black eyes widened in fear. "Let's be careful that none of them steal our precious son."

Duncan was silent. He felt a little ashamed of himself. But a nagging fear haunted him. *Will God reject me forever if I keep going farther into sin? I want to be saved sometime, but right now it is not possible. I am too deeply lost.*

His thoughts drifted to a lady he had met on the bike route last week. He remembered her lilting voice, "My name is Wilkister." He hadn't been able to forget her ever since. He liked to tease her to see her dimples.

The way of the Luo is to take many wives. This is a sign of great wealth. I can tell Wilkster is lonely and that she likes me a lot. Alseba is a wonderful wife, but I would like to have another one. So he reasoned with himself. But the guilt in his heart only increased.

chapter ten

To Add a Wife

As Duncan rode his bike to Ahero the next day, his thoughts drifted back to Wilkister. *Will I see her again today?* he wondered. *But why don't I simply take her as my second wife? Then I could enjoy living with her every day!*

As he waited with the other bike-taxi drivers at the junction, one of them asked, "Duncan, are you still seeing Wilkister?" Duncan nodded, and told them of his visit to her home. "Why don't you take dowry for her?" another man asked.

"I haven't taken dowry for Alseba yet," he replied. "It would be taboo to take cows for Wilkister before I pay Alseba's dowry."

They all nodded. "Why not just build a house for her?" someone suggested. "It's done all the time."

That's exactly what I want to do. Duncan sighed to himself. *She could stay in the cookhouse till I get a house built. But what would Mama Dolphine say?* He scratched his close-shaven head.

Just then a customer strode over to them for a ride. Duncan vied with the others for her business. She chose Duncan and haggled with him over the fare before he taxied her to her destination. Thus Duncan's day sped by as he hauled all manner of people and freight, although he spent several long spells of waiting for customers.

On the way back to Lela, he spied Wilkister returning from the pond with a bucket of water balanced on her head. He stopped to talk with her. Soon he lost all track of time. Before he knew it, the sun was setting in the rapid way it does near the equator.

"I must go home," he said. "Alseba will worry much. But remember the position I want to give you. You will receive many good things as my second wife. I am tired with Alseba, and I love only you. I wish I had taken only you in the beginning."

Wilkister's long lashes swept her cheeks as she smiled. "I will think on this word. I will answer you on Saturday."

"*Aaya*," (okay) Duncan shook hands with her and biked back to Lela. When he reached the dala, he heard the wail of a newborn child. *Oh, has Alseba given birth?* he thought excitedly. *Perhaps she has given me another son.*

He stooped to enter the mud hut, but was chased away by the midwife. "You have a daughter," she told him. "But do not enter to see her yet. Sit outside for a short time." Duncan sat down on the mud outcropping of the hut to wait. *Only a daughter,* he thought with disappointment. *But maybe Wilkister will give me a son.* He squirmed with guilt over the thought of his adultery. Soon the midwife stuck her head out the door and beckoned for him to enter.

This time he poked his head into the bedroom and found Alseba on their single bed, with a tiny baby. "Sorry I'm late," he told her. He didn't exclaim over the new baby as he might have, but just took a cursory glance and went outside again. Duncan wasn't able to face his wife. *What will she say when she discovers I have been unfaithful?*

The baby girl was weak and seemed to have trouble breathing. Alseba tended to her with a worried look on her face. Mama Dolphine, who had been caring for Otieno, kept the boy overnight.

That evening as Duncan lay in bed, his thoughts continued to trouble him, and sleep was slow in coming. *Oh, I know it's not right,* he agonized. *But I've entered too far into this sin to become free.*

"Turn to Jesus," a voice seemed to whisper. "You know what Mama

Dolphine has taught you. His blood will set you free." *But I already asked Wilkister to marry me,* he argued with the Holy Spirit. *I love her. I want her.* Having drowned the Holy Spirit's voice with his arguments, he soon fell asleep.

By morning the newborn had died. Alseba's wailing woke her husband. Mama Dolphine also came running to see what brought such grief. They buried the unnamed infant that day. Duncan tried to continue with life as usual, his anticipation of a new wife easing whatever grief he felt. But Alseba took it very hard and moped around the house morosely.

That Saturday Wilkister gave her answer as promised. "I will gladly come to be your wife, if Alseba doesn't mistreat me. Have you spoken to her about it?"

Duncan hung his head. "No. Just come. You can even come today, if you're not too busy." He stood tall. "I know Alseba won't quarrel about this, because she's a quiet person who accepts anything I say."

"*Aaya,* I'll get my things and come today. Can you carry for me my trunk? I will walk, but you must wait until I gather my things."

"No problem. I'll just wait here by the road." Soon he had the heavy trunk tied onto his bike rack with rubber strips. He zoomed along the path beside the road. Exhilaration gave him more energy, and he made it home in record time.

"Why are you home this time of the day?" Alseba asked in puzzlement. "And whose trunk is that on the back of your bike?" She seemed suspicious.

Duncan didn't know what to say. "I'm not home for good. Just brought someone's trunk." He swung his bike around. "Prepare for a visitor," he yelled over his shoulder.

"What kind of a visitor?" Alseba's shrill voice carried back to him across the path, but he didn't answer. She would know soon enough. He went back to Ahero, waving to Wilkister as she passed, carrying a handbag, on the way to his home. Alseba would surely accept this calmly.

The rest of the day could not go fast enough. But when he got home, things were not as he had imagined. Alseba met him at the door, her eyes throwing daggers. "What's going on?" she stormed. "This girl comes to my house and tells me she is your wife. I never thought you would become a polygamist. I thought your mother raised you better! You're not like the man I married. I'm leaving!" She pointed to her bag, packed and waiting on the floor of the main room.

"You are not going anywhere!" he shouted back. "You stay right here. If you go somewhere, I'll beat you."

Alseba stomped her small foot. "It seems the devil has gotten into you. I don't want to live with someone like that. I am done listening to you."

Duncan's eyes blazed, but he controlled his temper when he saw Wilkister's head peep out of Alseba's cookhouse. "Stay here," he commanded Alseba. "I will treat you as I treat Wilkister. Don't go." His voice became pleading. "At least wait until tomorrow. Think it over first."

Alseba's mouth pressed into a thin, straight line. She disappeared into the bedroom in a huff. Duncan was relieved she was not leaving tonight.

He went out to the cookhouse to meet his new wife. Soon they were laughing and talking together.

Without warning, a broad, black form appeared in the door, blocking the sunlight. It was Mama Dolphine. "Duncan," she said in an ominous tone. "Come here." Duncan slunk out of the cookhouse and over to her hut across the yard. "Sit down," she told him. He sat, trembling, for he knew he was about to be lectured.

"Duncan, what have you done?" she entreated. "I took you off the streets, welcomed you into my home, and treated you like my real child. I've taught you the difference between right and wrong. Why did you do this?" Her gentleness took him by surprise.

"Mama Dolphine," he replied with a shrug, "This is not bad. I just took a second wife."

"Did you really do a good thing? Is she really your wife? Or have you committed adultery?" Mama persisted.

Duncan squirmed. "Maybe you don't think it's good. But, as I'm seeing it, all Luos are doing such things." He studied her white veiling. "I know in your church they teach you many strange things. People even say you worship devils." Mama Dolphine grimaced, but he went on. "However, I am not a part of your church. I don't need to keep your church rules."

"Duncan, these are not just church rules." Mama's eyes flashed. "This is the Word of God! You're going to have to answer to God some day!"

Duncan hung his head in shame. Then he jumped up and strode out of her large hut. He nearly tripped over Jaduong, who was lounging under the shade tree in the cool night air.

When he returned to his own hut, the smell of food enticed him to sit down at the table with Wilkister and wait for his supper. Soon Alseba entered with the *pi logo*. (water for washing hands) She slowly poured water from a pitcher into a basin as Duncan washed up. Then she returned, carrying a steaming round of *ugali* and a small plate of *sakumu*. The women left him alone with his meal, according to custom, while they returned to the cookhouse to eat their own supper. Wilkister was still considered a visitor, so Alseba prepared the meal alone. After all, it was Alseba's cookhouse. Tomorrow evening Wilkister would help her.

Apparently Alseba is going to welcome Wilkister in a good way, Duncan thought. Perhaps it was good he didn't know what would happen the next day.

chapter eleven

Curse

D UNCAN AWOKE THE NEXT MORNING IN THE COOKHOUSE. HE stretched, yawned, and sat up in bed. *I'm hungry,* he thought, and went outside to hunt for Alseba. He found her weeding in the field next to their home. *Good, it seems she has decided not to run away.*

"Why don't you make chai?" he demanded.

Alseba grimaced, but said nothing. Even though she walked submissively back to the house, her face resembled a thundercloud. Duncan pretended not to notice. After he ate a heaping bowl of *nyoyo* and drank two cups of chai, he entered the former cookhouse to tell his new wife good-bye.

"I'm leaving now. I'm going to work," he told Wilkister with a tender smile. "*E-e,* (here) money for food." He shook her hand in the cultural manner of the Luos and left for his bike-taxi job.

When Duncan returned to his dala late that night, he went straight to Alseba's little cookhouse where he had put the mattress for his second wife. All was dark and still. "Where's Wilkister?" he bellowed to Alseba, who was cooking the evening meal outside.

She stared at her toes. Hesitatingly, his wife replied, "She left."

Duncan towered threateningly over her. "She ... what? Did you quarrel with her? What has happened? Did you chase her?" Apparently Alseba was not going to say more. She just ignored him and began stirring the bubbling pot of *ugali* with all her might.

Duncan's fury erupted, and he slapped her face. She stepped back a few paces and set her hands on her small hips. "If you want a ripe *ugali* tonight, you must leave me alone. If you disturb me, it is going to burn. Be quiet with your stupid questions. If you want to know anything, go see your beloved Mama Dolphine." Then she gave her full attention to the mound of *ugali*, using both hands on the wooden stir-spoon as the mixture became thicker.

Duncan had always liked her spunk before. But when he was the recipient, it was different. "Don't talk to me that way!" he yelled, taking down the heavy hoe from where the blade was stuck between the roof and the wall. When Alseba saw what he was doing, she froze in fear. Then she stuck the *ugali* spoon in the bubbling pot and ran out the door.

Duncan had no problem catching up with her. He grabbed her roughly by her shoulder. "I am your husband; you are my property. You will not speak disrespectfully to me. You chased Wilkister, didn't you?"

He could see the fear in Alseba's eyes. She eyed the sharp-bladed hoe he carried. "Yes," she replied. "But don't beat me!"

"You dare to chase away my second wife and then ask me not to beat you! As if you deserve any mercy! I am going to teach you a lesson." Duncan was furious.

He hoisted the hoe as Alseba tried once more to flee. Just then, Mama Dolphine appeared in the doorway of her hut. No doubt she had been watching all this time. Duncan lowered the hoe and slunk back to his house. He looked over his shoulder to see Alseba collapse under the mango tree and burst into tears.

Duncan was too ashamed to face Mama Dolphine just now. He slunk into his own hut. Slowly he dropped into the one-armed chair and tried to calm down. He attempted to justify himself, but when his rage had fully subsided, he began to feel guilty.

That was a terrible way to act, Duncan admitted to himself. *I was so angry! If Mama Dolphine had not appeared, I would've hurt Alseba.* Although Duncan felt guilty, he was too ashamed to say so to either Alseba or Mama

Dolphine. He put his head in his hands. He felt so miserable he wanted to poison himself, but he quickly dismissed the thought.

Duncan slept in the cookhouse alone that night and let Alseba have the bed in the house without saying a word to her.

The next morning, Duncan decided he needed some answers from Mama Dolphine. He was too ashamed to speak to Alseba just yet. Duncan walked over to Mama Dolphine's hut. "*Hodi*," (knock, knock) he called politely.

"*Donji*," (come in) she replied. "What is it?" But Duncan could tell she knew precisely why he had come. "Sit down," she invited.

Duncan did not sit. Instead, he paced around agitatedly. "Where is Wilkister? Why did Alseba quarrel with her?" His guilt and turmoil creased lines in his forehead.

Mama Dolphine sighed. "They beat a very loud noise about some money, and Alseba caned Wilkister. She chased your second wife away with bad words. Duncan, why do you not learn? The way of sin always ends up in trouble. You almost hurt Alseba. That was a terrible sin. You know it is wrong to take another wife. It's called adultery. I've taught you all this, so why should you be surprised when things go bad for you? Sin has its payment. Because you did this, no peace will stay in your home."

Duncan stepped back. But he replied obstinately, "You say this is adultery, but that teaching is just from the white man's culture. According to Luo culture, polygamy is acceptable."

"Don't I know that?" Mama shot back. "Remember, I have stayed as a Luo for a longer time than you. I know my Bible better than you. God's commandments were not first given to a white man. They were given to the Jews, but his laws are for all people. Even if polygamy is according to Luo culture, it is not right."

Duncan didn't know what to say, he was so angry. He knew her words were true, and they condemned him. "You quit preaching to me!" he lashed out. "You talk of worshipping God, but we all know you people are just blood suckers who worship demons. I don't want to hear anymore of your words."

Just then he noticed a bent form sitting outside the hut on its mud ledge. Jaduong rose and stood in the doorway, blocking most of the light. "What you said," he barked, "was not good. You have not yet learned to speak with fear to your elders." His bushy white brows knit together ominously. "Your words were taboo. Do not talk like that to my wife!"

Duncan tried to hide his surprise. *Jaduong is defending Mama Dolphine.*

The old man went on. "You will pay for what you said." Abruptly he turned and huffed away like a tornado cloud.

Mama Dolphine sighed. "I don't know what he's going to do." They both knew Jaduong could be dangerous when angered. Duncan froze inside as he wondered what revenge the old man might plan.

Wilkister returned to their home two days later. Duncan's shame and stubbornness still kept him from speaking to Alseba. Even if he was embarrassed, he didn't want to make amends. He gave all his meager earnings to his second, favored wife. Alseba would have starved had it not been for her small business of selling soap and *mandazis*. (doughnuts without glaze) Duncan knew Mama Dolphine helped her out occasionally. Every night Duncan had trouble falling asleep because of the guilt that plagued him.

After a week, Duncan forgave Alseba and began supporting her again. But he was facing hard times financially. One evening he complained to Wilkister. "I'm not finding many people to carry on my bike-taxi job. I don't know how I'm going to feed another baby," he said, referring the small life growing within his second wife.

"The sun burned our maize too," Wilkister replied with a sigh. "You know hail destroyed our rice. It almost seems like someone put a curse on us."

The suggestion gave Duncan a jolt. "Do you suppose Jaduong got his revenge?" he wondered aloud.

"What revenge?" Wilkister asked innocently.

"Well, one day I angered him by something I said to Mama Dolphine. He vowed to pay me back. Perhaps he paid the witchdoctor to put a curse on me."

Wilkister's eyes widened with fright. "It will take many sheep to pay a good witchdoctor to take away that curse." Both remembered they owned no animals.

Everything is so hopeless, Duncan despaired. *I thought when I took the second wife it would be the beginning of a wonderful life. I thought it would make me a great man in the eyes of the Luos. But this decision has brought me only grief.*

Quickly he glanced at Wilkister. She must not know what he was thinking. But she was still pondering the curse. "The neighbors also lost their crops," she pointed out. "Maybe it wasn't a curse after all."

"Probably the curse was a powerful one that affected our neighbors as well," said Duncan. "You remember Jaduong harvested a lot of rice." Wilkister nodded thoughtfully.

Duncan talked to Alseba about the possibility of a curse on them. She replied wisely, "If you think it is a curse, why not ask Mama Dolphine? Perhaps she will tell you what you could do to have Jaduong pay a good witchdoctor to lift the curse. You spoke in a hurry when you were angry. Can you tell him 'sorry'? Would this make the anger of your father disappear?"

Duncan winced at her suggestion. It would be hard on his pride. "You know I love my mother and I spoke without thinking. I don't want to speak of this anymore, but I am ready to do almost anything to be prosperous again," he admitted. Alseba said nothing more about the matter.

As Duncan lay in bed, he agonized, *I can't talk about this with Wilkister because I don't want her to know what I quarreled with Mama Dolphine about. I know Alseba gave good advice, but this will be difficult. What am I going to do?*

chapter twelve

A Plot to Kill

WHEN DUNCAN RETURNED FROM HIS JOB, HE SAW HIS WIVES HAD finished chopping down the field of maize stalks. He wandered into the cookhouse where he found them preparing their evening meal. He pulled up the stool Wilkister offered him.

"You know that I think Jaduong has placed a curse on the land we farm," he said abruptly as Wilkister sat on the floor. "I've been wanting to migrate. This will take money, and if we don't have a good harvest, I cannot start my own dala outside Jaduong's land."

Alseba spoke first, as befitted the senior wife. "It is true. The maize was burned by the sun. The rice crop was also destroyed. We saved no money."

Wilkister wondered aloud, "Will Jaduong give you a piece of his land, really? Will he divide it between you and Pius, or will Pius get it all?" The unspoken thought hung in the air, *Jaduong has never accepted Duncan and will not give him land.*

Alseba took the liberty to reply to her co-wife, "We know Jaduong is at odds with all of us. What are you thinking? Are you thinking he will give us more land while he has put a curse on the land we already farm?"

Wilkister's eyes flashed. "Just *ling'.* (be quiet) I was only asking whether Jaduong had a plan to split his land before the witchdoctor's curse. And I was not asking you, I was asking our husband."

Duncan frowned and held up his hands. "I know for certain Jaduong has no plan of giving me a piece of his land. I've been checking the prices of land around here. We can afford a small land, but not if our crops fail. We need maize and beans to eat during dry season. And I must have the money from the rice farm if I am going to save anything," he stated solemnly. He looked to Alseba to hear what she had to say.

With her hands folded primly in her lap and her eyes lowered respectfully, she said, "As I told you before, I think you should ask Mama Dolphine if, in fact, Jaduong put a curse on our land. And if he was angry because of your bad words, why don't you apologize and request him to pay the witchdoctor to lift the curse?"

Duncan nodded in acknowledgement, but did not reply immediately. Then he turned to Wilkister.

"I have no more words," she told them. "Alseba's advise is wise."

Duncan decided to follow through with his first wife's plan. Even if he no longer cared for her romantically, he recognized the wisdom of her recommendation. That evening after Mama Dolphine and Jaduong had eaten their evening meal, Duncan saw Jaduong go out to rest under the mango tree. Duncan came to the doorway of Mama Dolphine's house. "*Hodi*, he said politely.

"*Donji*," Mama answered. "Have a seat." She offered him some *ugali*, but he shook his head.

"I have come to you to speak to you of something important," he told her after shaking hands. She looked at him expectantly, so he went on, "You have seen our shriveled maize stalks that were burned by too much sun. We got very little maize. Birds have eaten most of our bean seeds, so we harvested no beans either. Moreover, hail destroyed the rice crop. We are just thinking the witch doctor put a curse on us." Duncan watched Mama's face carefully, but she did not blink. "Do you know anything about this?" he asked finally.

"No," she replied, but Duncan didn't take her word for it. She wasn't looking him in the eye.

Duncan decided to be very direct. "Did Jaduong hire the witchdoctor to put a curse on our land? Was Jaduong angry with the way I spoke to you the day Wilkister came?"

Mama Dolphine laughed with embarrassment about the events of that day. "Why do you come to me? Just ask Jaduong." Clearly she was afraid of telling anything.

"Mama, you can trust me," Duncan said earnestly, taking her hand. "I must have this curse lifted, if it is indeed so. I am willing to do anything, but I have no money to pay the witchdoctor."

Mama Dolphine shook off his hand. "Please talk to Jaduong. If you tell him sorry for your disrespectful words on that day, maybe he will leave his anger. Perhaps if you offer to work in his fields, he will even pay the witchdoctor himself, so your land will be productive once more. I only ask you not to speak of me in your conversation with Jaduong."

Just then Jaduong's form blocked the dusky light remaining in the doorway. They both gave a start.

"I have heard the words you said," said Duncan's stepfather in his matter-of-fact way. He didn't sound angry. Duncan gave a small sigh of relief. Jaduong sat down slowly. "Mama Duncan," he addressed his wife in the respectful manner of the Luo, "Do not fear. It is good that Duncan knows why his crops do not bear." He turned to Duncan, his bushy eyebrows rising threateningly. "Are you really sorry for your bad words? Or do you just want your land to become productive again?"

Duncan squirmed. "I am truly sorry, sir," he replied. "I spoke hastily with anger. I love my mother very much, and I do not speak to her like that when in my right mind. I ask for your forgiveness, Jaduong." He purposely didn't mention his land.

"Will you promise to help me weed and harvest my next maize crop?" asked Jaduong.

"So that you may do what in return?" asked Duncan.

"So that I may forgive you," barked Jaduong.

"And then?" Duncan prompted again. But Jaduong was silent, apparently not desiring to speak more on the subject.

Duncan tried not to let his anxiety show. "Jaduong," he said, "If I help you with your maize field, will you pay the witch doctor to lift the curse? I have no money. The witch doctor will require at least a ram in payment."

"I will give you money, if you repay it," Jaduong said at last. "If you fail to pay me back by next harvest time, I will have the curse put back on you."

Duncan shuddered. *We must get a good harvest this time! If it is not like that, I fear the next curse will be much worse.*

"Aaya," Duncan agreed. I will pay back this loan by harvest time. If I don't pay, I know maybe the curse will be placed back on my land."

With handshakes all around, the agreement was made. Jaduong shuffled out of the hut, and Duncan took this as his signal to leave. He wanted to say more to Mama Dolphine, but this was not the time. When he stood up, he took her hand. "Thank-you," he said simply. She nodded, her eyes speaking volumes of love and sympathy.

His wives were elated when he told them the good news. Their relief shone from their eyes. When he exited the hut and sat on the ledge outside, he smiled to hear them jabbering excitedly to each another. *It seems they get along sometimes,* he told himself. *Truly, I'm also happy. It sets my heart at rest, because I've given my 'sorry' to Jaduong. I'm even happier, knowing the curse will be taken off my land.*

But that night when he went to the cookhouse to be with Wilkister, he couldn't relax as his conscience plagued him about his adultery. *I'm a sinner,* he admitted to himself. *But I can't seem to help myself.* In his misery, it didn't occur to him that there was hope for his future. He didn't know Mama Dolphine was praying for him.

One day when Duncan was transporting a young man to his destination in Koroe, he heard a group of men's voices yelling excitedly from inside a bar. "Stop here," the man on the back of his bike said. "What is happening?"

Both of them walked into the filthy joint. Duncan stepped up to the animated group, and picked up snatches like "Bloodsuckers.... Americans.... kidnap children.... suck people's blood."

Maybe they are talking about Mama Dolphine's church, he decided. *This word has spread far. I know it's not true, but even me, I've passed on this word to many people. Mama Dolphine told me the rumors began when the church was founded eight years ago.*

Duncan pressed through the mass of bodies into the inner circle where he could hear the discussion more clearly. A fiery-eyed man insisted, "We must kill these people before they kidnap any more children!" Cheers erupted. "Kill them!" the drunken men shouted. "Shed the blood of the bloodsuckers!"

Not everyone in the bar was drunk. The ringleader seemed sober, as did a number of other men--Duncan's friends--who were all planning their wicked scheme. *If these men are having such an exciting plan, even me, I will join them,* Duncan decided in the heat of the moment.

"When the missionary drives to the interior, we will slash him to death and burn the vehicle," the clan leader announced in his authoritative way. Loud cheers erupted from the drunken men, and the sober men nodded in assent.

Duncan's brain whirled. "We should save kerosene and bring jugs of it to where the missionary pastor often goes," he heard himself say. "It must be far from the road, where no one can find us. Then we can burn him and his vehicle." The drunken men cheered again.

The clan leader scratched his head importantly. "These kidnappers must be eliminated by all means. This sounds like a good plan."

"Let's collect drums of kerosene!" one man suggested. "Then we can burn them and their vehicle." They laughed drunkenly. The men planned to put roadblocks in place to keep the missionary's vehicle from escaping. Would their victim fall prey to their scheme? Would he cooperate with their plans?

chapter thirteen

Salvation at Midday

ONE MORNING, AS DUNCAN AND PIUS SAT DRINKING CHAI IN MAMA Dolphine's house, they heard a vehicle drive by. Pius smiled and helped himself to another handful of *nyoyo*. "It's the vehicle of the pastor," he told Duncan. "I've washed that Safari many times." And he went on with his chai.

Duncan's lip froze over his cup. He set the chipped enamel cup down. Jumping up, he hurried to the window to look out. Then he strode outside and swung onto his bicycle. Without a good-bye to his wives, he drove away to the prearranged meeting place. *This is the day we will kill the missionaries! I helped pay for that gasoline,* he reminded himself. Duncan joined the clan leader and his friends where they stood making final plans to lynch the pastor.

Suddenly a little neighbor boy ran up to them. "Fred Owino was gored by a bull last night," the boy gasped. "The white man is coming to take him to the hospital!"

The tall, proud clan leader's lips curled. He clapped his hands. "This is our chance!" he exulted. "Let's set up those stones like we planned, so that we can prevent the missionary and Fred from returning. Have you been collecting kerosene to torch the vehicle and burn those blood-sucking devil worshipers?" Duncan and a few of the others nodded, and they tallied the amount of fuel they had stockpiled.

The Safari returned around noon. After it reached Fred's house, a white man and another Luo, probably a Christian from their church, carried the hurt man inside. Duncan waited in the bushes with his other neighbors. A few men blocked the road with rocks and thorns. When the two men pulled away in the Safari, the road-bock apparently confused them. They stopped and the African emerged from the vehicle.

Duncan smiled at the clan leader, who rubbed his hands with glee. Something evil stirred in Duncan's heart. The Luo man asked directions from a group of women. They shrilly shouted, *"Jachienja, Jachienja!"* (devil; blood sucker) The national jumped back in, and the Safari took off. It deviated from the blocked path and crossed an earthen wall from a dry rice field paddy, scraping its bottom.

Duncan crept through the trees with the others. He saw his friends running toward the Safari. They brandished clubs, machetes, and rocks. The vehicle stopped. A bearded white man, apparently disoriented, jumped out and tried to stop the people from coming closer.

Duncan wanted to earn the clan leader's pleasure. He ran with his club and struck the tall white man. Strangely, the *misungu* seemed to feel no pain.

Duncan watched his friend Sampson bash a club over the American's head. The man clutched his eye, then, in confusion, fumbled blindly for something on the ground. He stumbled into the vehicle as though guided by an Unseen Hand.

He crossed over to a group of men who were surrounding the vehicle. The two Christians climbed out again. Duncan saw his friend from Kobongo raise his machete as if to strike.

Something Duncan could not explain made him march over and push the scowling Luo away. He didn't understand why the Christians' hapless state changed the anger in his heart to pity.

"Get into the vehicle and go away," Duncan hollered at the bleeding man, not quite knowing why he was switching sides in this war. He added in the Luo language, "Turn left and you will reach the road after one hundred yards." Although the Luo man understood what Duncan said, he didn't seem to believe him, for he said nothing to the pastor.

The Safari crept back to the dry rice field as Duncan's friends broke its windows with clubs and rocks. The crowd grew quickly as the frenzied cries increased.

The passengers alighted from the vehicle once more, not knowing which direction to go. Duncan's stomach lurched as he watched the Christian Luo sustain several blows on the back of his head with the flat of a machete.

Then Duncan waved the crowd away with authority he didn't know he possessed. Somehow Duncan wanted to save the lives of the missionary and the Christian Luo. *Peace shines from their faces,* he thought. *These men don't deserve death, but their attackers are so cruel. They want to kill the Christians because of jealousy.*

But Duncan couldn't keep the bloodthirsty mob at bay for long. Before too long they advanced and began beating their innocent victims again. Their persecution continued off and on for the next two hours, as they vainly tried to kill them. The suffering saints seemed to feel no physical pain. Duncan wished he could do something to erase the look of trauma on the faces of the would-be martyrs as the crowd yelled and chanted. The mob seemed to enjoy the sight of blood.

Suddenly Duncan gasped. There was Jaduong! *What is he doing here?* Duncan wondered. *Will he help me save their lives?* But Jaduong yelled angrily, "What are you trying to do? Why don't you just finish them?"

Duncan sighed in disgust. He was glad Jaduong didn't spot him in the crowd. Duncan's friends fired questions at the Christian Luo, who had sustained the worst injuries. The national was so frightened he answered the crowd in falsetto.

The bearded white man spoke in English, but Duncan only understood the word "America." The crowd seemed to quiet when they heard that word, which symbolized wealth and power.

The missionary gestured with his hands, his eyes and smile communicating his love. *Why are we beating these good people?* Duncan wondered.

As Jaduong and the clan leader roped the Christians together, Duncan felt very helpless. A group of curious children pushed to the front to watch the Christians where they sat, securely bound. Duncan saw the crowd grow calm as the Christians sang for the children "Faith of Our Fathers" and "Jesus, Keep me Near the Cross." The mob paused to listen.

After a while, the clan leader got Duncan's friends stirred up again. They began yelling and screaming like the bloodthirsty men they were. Jaduong told the bound men to stand, which was difficult because of the ropes binding them.

Close by was a reed mat, a blanket, and other burnables. The clan leader torched the grass behind the vehicle with fuel Duncan had helped buy. He sloshed the kerosene all over the vehicle. Duncan clutched his throat in remorse at his part in this murder plot.

Duncan ran to a nearby bush and retched. *Oh, what have I done! God, this sin! Can you save me now?* he cried out silently. The windows of heaven opened to Duncan. He felt peace, as though God had reached down His hand and lifted him to heaven above. *I forgive you,* a still, small Voice whispered to his heart.

Sampson and Jaduong had let the air out of the tires on the far side of the vehicle. Duncan's smile froze as the Safari leaned towards the captives. They staggered to their feet.

As if in a dream, Duncan heard himself pleading with his friends not to lynch them. Someone lit the diesel-doused Safari. The mob tried once more to drag the Christians into the flames. Duncan sensed someone must be praying for them. Something stronger than Evil was keeping the Christians from being killed.

Duncan realized he couldn't help the Christians anymore. It would take Someone much more powerful than he was. *God, if You save them, I'll serve You the rest of my life,* he prayed desperately. As if in a daze, he watched the crowd separate the two bleeding men from the burning vehicle.

Sampson walked up to the bearded man and tried to provoke him by lightly whacking him. The missionary smiled lovingly. Sampson's evil laugh sounded like he thought this was great sport. The crowd grew angrier as the

Safari burned hotter.

Duncan thought, *Can anyone see the burning Safari from the road and tell the police? Small chance! This is so far from the road. Eee, but God can use this tragedy for His purpose. I feel guilty for helping to bring about this terrible thing.* But somehow, at that moment, he knew he was forgiven. Sweet peace washed over him.

The crowd became more edgy. Duncan could see the Christians were giving up. He wished he could do more, but he thought the pair must be almost dead. Blood continued to flow from their various wounds. He considered leaving.

Someone untied the Christian Luo as the mob prepared to kill him first. Duncan gave a start. *Aaii! What's that?* A maroon vehicle bounced toward them over the ruts from the dry rice paddies. *It's a mission vehicle! Someone has come to save them!* But when Duncan saw there were police inside, he ran away, frightened like the others.

The police chased the crowd and made arbitrary arrests. Duncan was among those who would be taken to Kodiaga, the most dreaded of prisons in Kisumu. He would have to wait for his sentence with the rest of the prisoners. *I know I will die there*, thought Duncan. *Has Jesus really forgiven me? Will Mama Dolphine's prayers for me be answered? Am I really saved?*

chapter fourteen
Imprisoned

DUNCAN CRINGED AS HE WAS SHOVED WITH SIXTEEN OTHER MEN INTO the filthy prison cell. The stench from the pile of waste in one corner made him gag. Seemingly there had been no provision for sanitary needs. A uniformed guard herded the prisoners with his *runga* (knobbed stick used for beatings) and made them sit on the cement floor. Soon another guard came in and demanded that each prisoner remove his shirt. They also surrendered their left shoes, according to prison rules.

Duncan shivered. *Oh God, do You care*? he cried out silently. *Did you really save me when I prayed today?* A calm peace and assurance told him Jesus did care, no matter what terrible things he had done and no matter what situation he was in.

The other prisoners, ill tempered, cursed each other and God. "I did nothing wrong," squawked one man. "I was only one of the onlookers!" Duncan recognized him and knew it was true. As he studied their faces in the semi-darkness, he could pick out about five or six he knew had helped with the beating. But most of them were innocent.

In the following days, Duncan scarcely knew how he survived. The food ration allotted to the prisoners was barely edible. Some days the beans were only half-cooked. Bugs floated around in the soup they were served one day. Two of the prisoners became seriously ill because of the unsanitary conditions. Several more caught colds from the dampness and lack of clothing. *Thank You, Lord, for preserving my health,* Duncan prayed daily.

Sometimes Mama Dolphine visited Duncan at the prison when she was in Kisumu to shop at market. Occasionally, she brought him small gifts of soap or food. "Thanks," he would say, embarrassed that she saw the horrible conditions in which he was forced to live.

Duncan tried to make friends with a few of the men by speaking kindly to them and sharing the gifts Mama Dolphine brought him. However, most of them were surly. "Leave me alone," one grouchy man barked as Duncan tried to start up a conversation.

After about a month, some of the prisoners gradually noticed there was something different about Duncan. They began speaking more courteously to him, especially when they saw his unselfish care of two men who were sick with typhoid.

"Why do you help us?" asked Okal, who was so sick Duncan feared he would die.

Duncan gave him a drink of tepid water. "I want to be like Jesus, who kindly forgave me even though I was a great sinner." Though he had received very little Bible instruction in his life, Mama Dolphine's teaching continued to pervade his mind. Duncan was amazed at the change the Lord had made in his heart and lifestyle.

When Okal died, Duncan wept. He felt sure the other sick man, Owino, would be next. The prisoners received little or no medical care other than what kind relatives could provide. Most of their families were too poor to make the trip to Kisumu to visit them and give them aid.

Time went on, and the Christians who had been beaten visited the prisoners occasionally and brought gifts of soap or food. He was surprised they wanted to help the prisoners rather than press charges. Their wounds were healing nicely, and they seemed to harbor no ill will.

One day Duncan was ecstatic to receive a small booklet with Luo Scriptures from the missionaries. "Thank you, thank you," Duncan said, cradling the holy Book. The guard only grunted and turned to exit and lock the door. The other prisoners didn't seem as interested in this gift as in some of the other offerings they had been given. But they had little to do, and sometimes Duncan looked up from his reading to see others likewise engrossed in their booklets.

Duncan received much spiritual food from the Gospels. He grew even kinder, and his Christlike spirit spoke to his fellow inmates. When two other prisoners received Christ, Duncan's cup was brimming over with joy.

Often he chafed at his imprisonment. He didn't deserve to be incarcerated since he had defended the would-be martyrs. He longed to see Alseba, Wilkister, and Otieno. He especially missed Mama Dolphine. He was ready for a good talk with Pius—and even missed Jaduong a little. *Lord*, he would pray, *may they release us soon!* He was afraid to stay in the cell too long, for he could easily get sick from the wretched conditions.

One day, he told Mama Dolphine he had accepted Christ. Her face glowed. "Praise the Lord! My prayers for your soul are answered at last! I will continue to pray for the day when you can escape this terrible place."

The next day, Owino died. Duncan's sorrow was tempered when he remembered the prayer of repentance the desperately sick man had prayed. Now Owino had gone to glory, where there was no more suffering.

Rumors drifted to the prisoners that the missionaries were trying to free them. The other prisoners were likewise astounded that those who were beaten weren't even going to press charges.

They all had to appear in court, but the judge didn't call the case that day. It was postponed several times. Maybe the judge was hoping for a bribe, but none of the destitute prisoners or their relatives had anything to offer. The white missionaries didn't offer a bribe either.

Finally, the day came when their case was called again. They all sat to be gaped upon by people in the packed courtroom. Duncan hung his head. *I know I stink, and I know I'm bony,* he thought. *This is so humiliating to have to sit here in handcuffs!*

He heard one of the white missionaries say something, and the scrawny man by his side interpreted softly for those who didn't know English, "He says they are not pressing charges, and they would like to see the prisoners released."

"Why aren't the missionaries wanting to pay us back?" one prisoner wondered. The others craned their ears to hear Duncan's answer.

In a whisper he replied, "They have told me Christians return good for evil and allow God to repay their enemies." The prisoners were amazed to hear this.

The judge hammered his gavel. All the prisoners were released. Duncan didn't know what to do or say. He could hardly believe it! The other prisoners were ecstatic.

Duncan bowed his head. *Father, thank You for setting me free—not only from my sins, but also from this prison. Please help me to live the remainder of my life for You. I devote myself to You anew.* Peace washed over his soul. He knew he was released for a purpose. Now he would serve God with all his being!

Duncan went home with a thankful heart. Those from his dala welcomed him back with open arms. The ladies prepared a feast. First they served chai, *chapatis*, (flat bread like tortillas) and bread with margarine. Next, they brought chicken, *ugali*, rice, *sakumu*, and potatoes. "I don't deserve this honor," he protested to Mama Dolphine.

"Yes, you do," she said. "You've been gone for many months, and we want to show our pleasure to have you back again! No one is more thankful than me, for I've loved you the longest, and I am the only one here who rejoices in your salvation."

In the following days, Duncan found his strength returning, and he gained back some weight. He began attending church. After a few Sundays, the pastor wanted to help Duncan get his marriage straight. "You and Alseba are living in sin because you neither took dowry for a traditional marriage nor had a wedding," the pastor explained. "Wilkister is not really your wife either," he explained.

He arranged to take the young couple to Alseba's home, since it was necessary to have her parent's signatures on the marriage forms. After the meal there, they began having what the Luos termed dialogue.

"How can I agree to sign the papers if Duncan has never brought dowry?" the clan elder asked gruffly. Duncan agreed to try to bring a cow and some money whenever he could afford it.

After being published in the church for the required three Sundays, Duncan and Alseba were joined in a simple ceremony by the bishop. Mama Dolphine was the witness for Alseba, while Pius stood up for Duncan. Their only audience was two other couples whose marriages were legalized the same day.

On the way home from the legalization, Duncan felt renewed discomfort with having Wilkister as his second wife. He had heard the *misungu* pastor preach against polygamy on more than one occasion. Not only that, but after what he heard one morning in instruction class, he was convicted about making restitution for the things he had stolen.

A week later, he approached the pastor for counsel after the Sunday morning church service. "Pastor," he sighed. "I have a problem. My brother and I stole a lot of money from you missionaries. We took about 60,000 shillings. I'm very sorry."

He watched the pastor's eyes widen. "So you are the ones who robbed us!"

Duncan shivered. "You won't take us to court for that, will you? None of that money is left."

"No. Remember, we believe in allowing God take care of those who treat us wrongly. We don't repay evil for evil. I forgive you for this."

"Oh, thank you," Duncan breathed. "But you taught us in church today that we must repay what we have wrongly taken from people. How can I do this? I have no money. Since I returned from prison, I have many debts to pay because my wives borrowed a lot of money. Also, I am owing Jaduong a ram for paying the witchdoctor for me. I know I've told you about that thing."

"Don't worry," the pastor reassured him. "You can wait till after you harvest your rice, and then give what you can. After your maize harvest, do the same. We won't require you to pay back everything, but at least enough to show you want to make restitution."

Duncan breathed a sigh of relief. "Thank you, pastor. You are very kind."

Then he thought of something else. "You know, before I was saved, my brother Pius stole a bike for me so I could start my business. Is it wrong for me to own this bike?" He held his breath.

The pastor hesitated. "Did you know when you got the bike that it was stolen?" he asked.

"Yes," Duncan replied. "But I don't think he knows how to find the owner."

"It's never right to steal. Nor is it right to let someone else steal something for you. But under these circumstances, it's almost impossible to do restitution. Maybe you could talk to Pius about it. If he ever finds the owner, you could pay him back gradually."

Duncan nodded. He doubted the owner could ever be found. But if possible, he would try to repay him for the stolen bike. "I'm willing to pay," he said. *Good, that's taken care of.* A load was lifted from his shoulders.

Then he sighed, and his shoulders bowed again under a new load of guilt. "Pastor, You know I'm a polygamist. I always knew it was wrong. But since I started attending church, I know I need to take care of this sin. According to your teaching, having two wives is wrong. What should I do? I want what's right. I also want to be free to enter the instruction class."

"Yes, polygamy is wrong," the pastor agreed. "You must put Wilkister away. Your first wife is your only wife in the sight of God. Any other wives are just a form of adultery. In God's sight, there is only one husband and one wife. Send Wilkister away. She should not live with you."

Duncan shook his head. "But that's impossible in our culture. I have never heard of anything like this happening. We must stay with our wives. I don't know how I can send Wilkister away."

The pastor stroked his beard thoughtfully. "Since you are a Christian, you must follow the Bible, not Luo culture," he explained. "I see no other way out of this except to put away the adulterous woman."

"Please pray for me." Duncan's voice was forlorn.

"Yes, I'll pray for you," the pastor replied. "In fact, would you like me to pray with you now?" Duncan nodded. They bowed their heads together, and the pastor led out,

"Heavenly Father, we thank You for Duncan and that he has made his peace with You. Now be with him as he tries to make restitution for the money he stole. Lord, You know all things, and You have the power we need. Give Duncan this power to put away his second wife. Show him how obedience to your Word is more important than following Luo culture. Make all things possible to him through faith. In Jesus' Name I pray."

Tears flowed down Duncan's cheeks. "Almighty Father, thank You for saving me. Thanks for Your power. Please help me pay back the money I owe. And show me what to do with Wilkister. Amen."

Duncan felt better, but he still wasn't sure how all this was going to work.

Jubilee Market in Kisumu

fresh produce sold at market

women buying dresses

a mother gives her child *nyuka*

church service

baptism

national pastor

feet washing

choir

ordination service

rice fields

Kenyan potholes

a mother ties her child to her back

oxen pulling plow with rice fields in the background

donkeys carrying a load

oxen plow a rice field

funeral - a couple views the body for the last time

funeral - umbrellas provide shade

typical funeral fare -
ugali and intestines

grave site service

wash line in the yard of a *dala*

cattle are the wealth of the Luo

a Luo cook cuts wood with a
machete for her cooking fire

ugali made from millet with chicken

chai, bread and *chapatis*

a well is the main water source for those lucky enough not to haul water from a river

cooking over an open fire

a happy family

mud hut with small abode for animals

African laundromat

sweeping the floor with a whisk-broom

washing hands before eating *nyoyo*

a happy hostess serves chai with sweet potatoes

Building a house

bikes hauling wood

biker hauls grass

nailing together the framework

tying on the cross-pieces

getting ready to thatch the roof

women haul water to make mud which is used to fill in the walls

hauling mud to the house

filling in the walls with mud

a completed hut

bike taxi

receiving parcels for AIDS victims

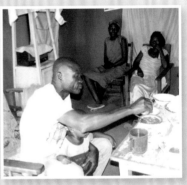

a polygamist and his two wives

sunset scene at Lake Victoria

Part Two

Transformed

chapter fifteen

The Matter of Wilkister

As the evening shadows lengthened, Duncan and Alseba retraced their steps home after a long day of hoeing maize. Duncan had planted two acres, so that meant lots of hard work. He dropped wearily onto the old, one-armed chair to await the evening meal. Alseba disappeared into her cookhouse to supervise Wilkister's supper preparations.

While Alseba helped her co-wife put the finishing touches on the meal, Duncan felt those familiar twinges of guilt. *I know I shouldn't have two wives,* he found himself thinking again. *But it's not the proper thing for a Luo to send his second wife away!*

The Holy Spirit whispered, "Wilkister is not really your wife in My sight. Send her away and tear down her house, as Pastor William advised."

Duncan felt miserable, torn between the Luo culture and what he knew was right. *No one has ever done this before,* he tried to reason again. But it was useless. Deep inside, Duncan knew he loved Wilkister too much to send her away. *Oh Lord,* he prayed in desperation. *Give me a desire to do what You want me to do! Give me strength and courage!*

Soon Wilkister came in with a pitcher and basin to wash his hands. No longer a visitor, she usually helped with the cooking under Alseba's direction. Alseba followed her co-wife with a large round of *ugali.* Then Wilkister reentered the hut with a plate of *sakumu*. Duncan thanked them, then his two wives went to eat in the cookhouse. Duncan ate hungrily, then washed his hands again in the basin.

The next day, Duncan rode his bike to Ahero to try to find some bike-taxi work. His family needed food. Besides this, he was trying to save some money for restitution to the missionaries, since he had repented of this theft. In the meantime, his wives could work on weeding the maize.

A week later, Pius met Duncan on the road home one evening. He surprised Duncan by saying, "I am going to Nairobi to get a job. Then I will send money for Mama Dolphine if there is any left after paying rent and food."

"I don't know if that's a good plan," Duncan told him honestly. "Most people who find work in Nairobi use all their pay for rent and food. Living costs so much in the city. Besides, there are many temptations. But if you will go, I hope you can find a good job. We will miss you."

They had reached the dala. Pius gave Duncan a happy salute before stepping into Mama Dolphine's hut for his evening meal.

"It's so hard to make money these days!" one of Duncan's bike-taxi friends grumbled a week later as they waited together for business.

"Yes, it seems there's no work," Duncan agreed. He settled himself to wait, possibly for hours. Just then, he was surprised to see the pastor's daughter walking towards them.

"I want to go to Kasongo," she told Duncan, after greeting him in Luo. Duncan was thrilled because now he could earn at least forty shillings. Maybe he could set some aside to give to Pastor William on Sunday. To Duncan's surprise, someone at Kasongo wanted a lift back to Ahero, so he was paid for his return trip as well. Seldom did he make this much money in one day.

When he arrived home that evening, his wives still hadn't returned from hoeing the maize field. He sat down on the mud ledge that surrounded the house to wait for them. Inevitably, when he had time to think, he felt convicted of his adultery.

Oh God, he finally prayed. *I am tired of living in sin. I know how I live doesn't please you. I've lost the peace and joy I found after I was saved. Oh, forgive me for taking a second wife! Please cleanse me with your blood. I promise to send Wilkister away. I will even tear down her house.* Sweet peace poured over Duncan's soul, and he knew he was forgiven. He joyfully began singing a Luo rendition of "There is Power in the Blood."

"Why are you so happy?" Alseba asked him as she and Wilkister walked toward the house. Their hoes were balanced over their heads, the metal blade hooked over their shoulders and the handles protruding behind them.

Duncan wasn't sure what to say. "I'll tell you and Wilkister tonight after we've eaten." He hesitated about his decision as he ate. Both he and Alseba would miss Wilkister if she left. Yes, the two wives fought now and then, and Alseba was always jealous of any attention Duncan gave her co-wife. But Wilkister was a good worker and a companion to Alseba. Was this really a wise choice? Then he shook his head. *I am not turning back,* he decided.

Duncan wondered what Wilkister would say when he announced his decision. Would she make trouble? His worry made the *ugali* and eggs taste like sawdust in his mouth. Finally he breathed another prayer, *Oh Lord, you see how troubled I am about sending Wilkister away. Show me how to do it. Give me the right words to say. And give me the strength to do it.* He swallowed the last mouthful of *ugali*, and washed his hands. Stepping into the cookhouse, he saw the women had also finished their supper.

He sat down on a water jug and took a deep breath. Abruptly he began, "Wilkister, I know in the Luo culture it is a good thing for you to be a second wife. I loved you when I brought you here, and I still do. However, polygamy is not a good thing for Christians." She lifted her head and sucked in her breath, but dared not look him in the eye.

Duncan went on, "I took you as my second wife before I was saved. But God's Word says His followers shouldn't do this. Alseba is my only true wife. Taking another woman is sin. So I need to put you away--you must leave."

Alseba's mouth dropped open. Then she shook her head in apparent amazement. When Duncan saw the understanding in her eyes, he wondered if she could tell how difficult this was for him.

But Wilkister stood up, her eyes flashing. "If you chase me, I will have nowhere else to go. My parents will not welcome me back again because I am your wife. They will only send me back to you. I will have no home. What can

I do?" Her words ended in a wail.

Duncan replied kindly, "I understand how you feel. I will not leave you with nothing like that. I'll give you money to go to Nairobi and payment for a month's rent. You can find a job there. Work is much in Nairobi." He had thought this through carefully, and he knew he'd have to borrow some money from Pius, who had chosen not to go to Nairobi after all.

Alseba bowed her head. But Wilkister shouted, "Duncan! How can you do this to me? You marry me, and after that you chasing me away because of the word you found in a white man's church. I thought you loved me!"

Duncan winced, and put his face in his hands for a moment. *Oh God, what am I doing?!* Then he found inner strength from on high. "Wilkister, I cannot have you as my wife anymore. It's sin. I can only love you as a fellow human being, not as a wife. I am not chasing you out into the dark and cold night. You can sleep here one more night—and in the morning, I will put you on a bus going to Nairobi." Duncan's gaze shifted from Alseba's glowing face to Wilkister's angry one. He motioned Wilkister to sit down.

Then Alseba spoke. "Wilkister, our husband has done a very good thing. He hasn't chased you away with a beating as many men might do because you did a taboo or upset him in some way. He is asking you to leave for good, but he is sending you away with a means of support. You can start a new life for yourself and your unborn child."

"Yes, Wilkister," said Duncan to the sullen woman, "I'm sorry for the way I wronged you by bringing you to my home as a second wife. In God's sight, you were never really my wife. And so you must go. Only, do not take a grudge against me to your grave."

Wilkister leapt to her feet and stomped outside. Duncan looked at Alseba, and a new surge of love arose in Duncan's heart for his one and only wife. "Alseba," he said tenderly, taking her hand. "No one will ever come between us again. I love you and you only as my wife."

Alseba's smile made her beautiful. "I am not one of those going to the white man's church, but many good things have happened to you since you began going there," she admitted. "You have become a much kinder man. And your beliefs led you to put away Wilkister, who offended me all this time. I want you all to myself."

"I'm glad," Duncan admitted. "That's the way it's supposed to be." They stayed in the cookhouse and talked for a long time. It reminded Duncan of the days when he was courting Alseba, and they used to have such long conversations that the other bike taxi drivers teased him about it.

The next morning after he drank his breakfast *nyuka*, Duncan asked Wilkister whether she had packed her bags.

"What bags?" she asked belligerently.

"You are leaving for Nairobi today," he reminded her. "I will not accept that you stay in my home any longer. Remember, we have been living in sin! Now I want to leave my sin. That means you must leave."

"I am not living in sin—I'm your wife. And I'm not leaving," she huffed back. Duncan was so angry he wanted to strike her. But he reminded himself he was now a Christian, so he just took a deep breath.

"Wilkister, you will leave," he repeated. "Do you want to go with your clothes, or do you want us to sell them?" Her eyes flashed, but seeing she had no other choice, she left to pack. When the lid on her trunk clattered down, Duncan and Alseba exchanged a sad smile.

Then he went to borrow the shillings he needed from Pius. "I don't know how soon I can repay you, but I promise to give it back sometime." Duncan hesitated.

"No problem," Pius reassured him. "I don't understand why you're doing this to Wilkister, but if you're sure it's the right thing to do, go ahead."

Just then Mama Dolphine returned from a week's journey she had taken to attend a funeral. "What's going on?" she asked when she saw Wilkister's sullen face and her packed trunk.

Duncan explained he felt convicted about his polygamy and was trying to set it right. "I'll tear down the house, too," he added, referring to the cookhouse Wilkister called her own.

Mama Dolphine rewarded him with a huge smile. "Oh, I'm so glad you're listening to the Lord's voice, Duncan," she encouraged. "You know I did not accept Wilkister living with you. Remember how we quarreled over it when she first came? Even God was not happy with your second wife. I hope she stays in Nairobi. And I hope she didn't bring any diseases to you."

Duncan gave a little start. He had never thought of diseases. The question of AIDS lingered in his mind, but he tried to shake it off. He went to give Wilkister a hand with her trunk. Soon they were on their way to Ahero. After he ushered her into a matatu bound for Nairobi and handed the conductor her fare, he told her, "Wilkister, good-bye. This is good-bye for good. I don't expect you to come back, okay? Reach well, and may God add you many good days in Nairobi." Then he rode away on his bike without looking back.

Thank You, God! he exulted as he pedaled home. *With your strength, I did my duty to Wilkister. I glorify Your name! Please help to follow through and tear down her house also, even if I know Alseba could use it as a cookhouse. That way all the neighbors will know I have left my sin completely.*

Waves of peace and joy flowed over him as he alighted from his bike and leaned it against his hut. He grabbed his hoe and headed for the maize field to join Alseba, singing as he went.

chapter sixteen

Hard Times

D UNCAN SAT UNDER A BIT OF HASTILY CONSTRUCTED THATCH supported by a thin pole. As he guarded the rice field from the birds that ate the full, plump heads of grain, he thought of the woman he had sent away.

Wilkister had already been gone over a month. Duncan wondered if she had found a job and a good room to rent. He thought of the debt he had incurred to give her a new start in Nairobi. Then he sighed. *It seems I can never save any money.*

Duncan looked up at the feathery, white clouds in the sky. *God,* he prayed, *I don't know what to do. All the money I earn from bike-taxi work is used to feed my family. And I need to save up to pay my debts to Pius and make restitution with the pastor.* His thoughts turned to prayer. *Oh, help me, God! Supply my needs.*

Then he remembered the Scripture he had read that morning. *It seems I read something about God caring for the grass, giving the lilies clothes, and feeding the birds. Wasn't the lesson something about putting our faith in God? He will take care of me!* Duncan felt a little better.

Just then Alseba came along to give him a break. "It looks like we'll have a good harvest!" she said brightly. Duncan only nodded. "What's wrong?"

she asked.

"We don't have any money now," he reminded her glumly. "I don't know how I will pay my debts. I still haven't repaid Jaduong for the ram he paid the witchdoctor to lift that curse. Now I owe Pius money too. How can I save? We use all the money I make for food."

"I know!" said Alseba. "Instead of eating meat once a week, we will eat only vegetables until the debt is paid off." She looked enormously pleased with herself.

I'm seeing she is happy, thought Duncan. *Maybe it has something to do with Wilkister being gone.* Out loud he said, "That is a good plan. I will set aside the money we normally use for meat to pay my debts and make restitution with the pastor." When Duncan mentioned restitution, Alseba frowned.

But he went on. "And hopefully, we will get a good rice harvest. I have another idea. Maybe if you would start a hotel business in Ahero, we could get more income."

"Where would you get the money to start with?" Alseba wondered.

Duncan sighed. "I'll just have to borrow more money from Pius," he admitted. "Let's think about it." He turned to walk slowly back to his dala.

As he entered the gate of his home, he gave a little start. Who was that sitting on the doorstep? When he got closer, his pulse raced as he recognized Wilkister.

"You are here," he remarked, trying to sound casual.

"I have come home," she replied. "How are you?" She fluttered her long eyelashes.

Duncan's heart skipped a beat. Then he noticed she was holding a baby, who strongly resembled him. "Wilkister, why did you come back?" he asked, trying to be stern. *This is not really my wife,* he reminded himself. But he picked up the baby anyway and held him. It was his child, no doubt about it. "Why aren't you in Nairobi?"

"There is no work in Nairobi. I had nowhere else to go," she replied with a woebegone look. Then Duncan noticed she wore an expensive dress.

"Where did you find money for your new clothes? How did you get money to return here?" he asked, his smile vanishing.

Wilkister looked away. "My money is gone," she answered at length, evading the question.

"It seems you have spent it on fine clothes and rich foods," Duncan said dryly.

Just then Wilkister eyed the spot where the cookhouse had stood. "Where is my house?" she demanded. She took her fussing son from his father's arms.

"You are no longer my wife," Duncan informed her. "I tore your house down and told you not to return. Why are you here?"

"I'm here because this is my home. I am your wife, Duncan." Duncan knew according to Luo culture it was true. He paced around, then walked away.

Oh God, he prayed. *I'm so discouraged. I began the day in a bad way because of the debt we have. Now Wilkister has returned.* It was as though the heavens were made of brass. Duncan did not receive an answer. Guilt for his wrong desires hung heavy upon him.

Then the bright idea came to him, *Why not go see Pastor William?* Duncan needed some counsel, and he knew the pastor would encourage him to do what was right. "Tell Alseba I went to Kisumu to see Pastor William," he told Wilkister as he left. "You are free to rest in the house. I will be back this evening."

Duncan swung onto his bike and began the long ride to Kisumu. When he arrived, the pastor's daughter welcomed him into the house and went to call to call her father from his office. Duncan was very happy that Pastor William was at home because he was often gone during the day.

"Duncan," he said, clearly surprised to see him. "How are you?" They shook hands in the customary manner of the Luo.

"Fine," Duncan replied. He tried to tell the pastor his problem in broken English mixed with Luo.

"Hmm," the pastor responded. "So you need money to send Wilkister home, but you have none." Duncan nodded. Pastor William stroked his beard, thinking hard. "Did you pay dowry for Wilkister?"

"No," Duncan replied. "It would be taboo, because I never paid dowry for Alseba."

The pastor smiled. "As a Christian, you no longer need to fear taboos," he reminded him. "But if you haven't paid dowry for Wilkister, might she not return to her home?"

"Yes," Duncan replied. "However, she said they would not welcome her at home anymore. They would send her back to me."

"Is this because of something cultural, or is it just something she said to keep you from chasing her away?" the pastor queried carefully. "And do you really want to send her home?"

Duncan squirmed. "Wilkister was just saying that, but I believed her because her family quarrels a lot. She has never lived in good agreement with them. As for me, I am having some longings for her." Pastor William gave a little start at Duncan's unusual honesty.

"Duncan, it is good you are admitting your desires. These longings you feel are very normal. The temptation itself is not sin. It's what you do with your desires that could put you in a deeper hole of sin and misery." Duncan listened intently, trying to understand some of the unfamiliar English words.

The pastor went on, "Please tell the Lord about your desires. This type of temptation you must run from. You need to send Wilkister away as soon as possible, because the longer she is there, the harder it will be for you. Why don't we take Wilkister back to her home, and we can sit down with the clan and explain why we are leaving her there? Perhaps they would agree if we did this."

"I'm seeing that as good," Ducan replied. He felt a burden lifting, especially after they prayed together. They arranged to go to Wilkister's home in a couple days when the pastor had an opening in his schedule.

In the morning while Duncan watched for birds, Alseba hoed in the maize field. In the afternoon, Duncan usually did bike-taxi work while Alseba chased the birds away in the rice field. In this way, he managed to save a small amount of money by the end of the week. *I'll give this to Pastor William when we go to take Wilkister home*, he decided.

He still saw Wilkister often, for Mama Dolphine was his next-door neighbor in the circle of huts. He often pled with God for strength to keep his thoughts pure.

The night before the pastor would come, Duncan went to Mama Dolphine's hut. "Mama," he said, "I am here to ask you to give Wilkister a word from me. Tomorrow Pastor William is coming here to collect her and me. We will go to her home and drop her there. We will have dialogue with the clan and hope they accept this word. Do you agree to tell Wilkister?"

"I agree," she said. "I have taken care of her needs, not because I wanted to, but because you asked me to. I will be glad when she is where she belongs."

"Even me," agreed Duncan. "It will be a relief to have her gone. Then she will no longer be a temptation to me."

Before the pastor came, Duncan bathed and dressed in his best clothes, though they were pitifully shabby. Then he went to get the money he would use to begin making restitution. He looked under his mattress. It wasn't there!

"Alseba," he called.

"*An*," (Here I am) she answered.

"Where is the money I was saving to pay Pastor William?"

She padded over to him, heavy with their third child. "I don't know. Where did you put it?" she asked.

But Duncan thought she looked guilty. "Here, under the mattress," he told her, showing her the empty spot.

"Maybe it fell beneath the bed," she suggested, then found a sudden excuse to go to the maize field.

"Alseba!" Duncan called. "Stay here. Where is that money?"

She couldn't look him in the eye. "I don't know," she replied.

"Did you use it for something?" asked Duncan, grabbing her shoulder.

"Don't grab me like that," she cried.

"Where is the money?" he demanded again, raising his voice.

Seeing there was no escape, Alseba cringed. "I used it to buy a dress for myself. I have only two dresses, and they are so tight. When I saw all of Wilkister's new clothes, I thought I could at least have one new dress. Please forgive me, Duncan!" She whimpered.

Duncan was angry but he tried to reason with her gently. "We were trying to save money to pay the debt, so we ate only vegetables. That was your thought. Why did you use the money for yourself?"

Alseba was crying by now. "I thought at first that you were going to use the money to pay Pius and Jaduong. But when I understood you were going to give it to the pastor, I decided to buy a dress for myself since I needed that more." Then she turned to face him squarely. "Why are you paying the pastor? You have no debt with him! I know you said you are doing restitution, but that seems foolish. I'm seeing you are just wasting money that we need."

Duncan fought to control his anger. *I'm saved*, he told himself. *I can't hurt my wife in my anger. I'll just have to forgive her. As a Christian, I must show her love and mercy.*

He took a deep breath. "Alseba, I feel you did wrong by using that money without asking me. But I see you do not understand why I wanted to pay the pastor. Also, you did need a new dress. Next time, just ask me if you need new clothes. I will be happy to buy you what you need if I can." Alseba blinked in surprise at his unexpected kindness. A bit embarrassed, she ducked out of the house.

Oh Lord, give us peace in this home! Duncan prayed. *Help me to love Alseba and respond to her in a Christian way!*

Just then Pastor William drove up. Duncan slunk over to the vehicle. When he reached the pastor's window, he asked politely, "How are you?"

"I'm fine!" said the pastor warmly. "All ready to go?"

"Yes," said Duncan, and climbed into the Cruiser. The thought occurred to him, *if Alseba had not taken it, I could give the pastor some money.* Then he remembered his promise to forgive her. *Lord, give me the power I need,* he prayed silently.

Wilkister had followed him and got in the back seat. Whatever she thought about what she had heard of the quarrel, Duncan didn't know. Had she seen Jesus in him and in his response to Alseba? he wondered.

chapter seventeen

Leaving the Past

DUNCAN SAT UNCOMFORTABLY ON THE PASSENGER SIDE AS THE Cruiser bounced over the rutted road. His discomfort stemmed from his heart, however, not from the rough ride.

"I asked a translator to go with us," the pastor informed Duncan. "Brother Francis will interpret." Duncan only nodded. Gloomily, he stared out the window at nothing in particular.

After Pastor William picked up Francis, they headed for Wilkister's home in Katito. It wasn't very far from Lela, and Duncan was thankful. He wanted this ordeal to end. He tried to forget his spat with Alseba. As they whizzed past Ahero, the whole issue weighed heavily on him. He realized he had not really forgiven Alseba for stealing the money, even if he had tried to respond kindly to her. His lingering anger weighed him down with guilt. The Spirit of God patiently prodded his heart, *Didn't I forgive all your sins? Shouldn't you forgive your wife?*

Stubbornly he argued back, *but she spent the money I wanted to use for restitution! She bought a dress when we needed more important things like food!*

God answered him, Duncan, which is more important? "All money is mine. I don't need the money you will pay for restitution. Peace with your wife is more important."

Duncan acquiesced. *Yes, Lord. I have sinned. I was angry. But I still think my wife did me wrong. I cannot forgive her in my own power.*

The Holy Spirit continued to speak to his heart. *My grace is sufficient for you. I forgave you. Forgive your wife, too. My power is yours. As I have forgiven her, so you must also do. Take My forgiveness as your own.*

Duncan's heart tingled. *God is going to forgive her through me? What—how? But He said His grace is sufficient for me.* Then he prayed, *Lord, I forgive her. I don't understand how You are taking my anger away, nor how this forgiveness is possible. But I forgive her. I do!"*

Sweet peace overflowed in his soul. He longed to talk to the pastor about it, but he didn't think Wilkister needed to know all the details.

Thank You, Lord! he praised as they drew near to the main gate of Wilkister's family home. *Thank You for setting me free from my anger. I'm sorry I grieved You with the bad words I spoke to Alseba. Thank You for keeping me from beating her. Show me how to demonstrate my forgiveness to Alseba.*

Pastor William turned off the Cruiser's engine and alighted. Duncan, Wilkister and the baby, and the interpreter followed the pastor into Wilkister's mother's house. The clan was expecting them, for they had sent word ahead.

First, the clan elders greeted their visitors by shaking hands or clapping in their faces and saying, "*Mirembe.*" (Peace) Many of them were *Rohos*, a traditional African religion mixed with Christianity. They wore white hats or veils and robes with a red cross on them.

Pastor William, Duncan, Francis, and Wilkister waited for several hours until the food was served. Duncan knew the clan was ignorant as to the purpose of their visit—for all they knew, the visitors had come to discuss dowry! At any rate, they wanted to serve their best. After bringing *pi logo*, (water for washing hands) the ladies carried in bowls of chicken, beef cubes, fried liver, *ugali*, rice, and *sakumu*. The clan members and visitors ate together in silence. Duncan gnawed at his meat with great relish, not knowing when he could afford to eat meat again.

After everyone had eaten, the dialogue began. Clan elders sat in a prim row along the left-hand wall, according to custom. The visitors sat on the right.

"Thank you for welcoming us like this," Pastor William began, waiting for his interpreter. "You have served us much good food. Now we have brought Wilkister back to your home again. You may keep her here." The white-haired men and old, wrinkled mamas lifted their eyes in shock. But the pastor went on, "Duncan took Wilkister to be his second wife. But he never took dowry, since he hadn't paid dowry for his first wife either." The clan members nodded. "Now Duncan is saved. He has realized it is sin to be a polygamist. We believe the Bible teaches that men are to have only one wife."

The oldest *jaduong*, (old man) with the longest, whitest beard held up a hand to interrupt him. "We are also saved, though we are worshipping in another church. But we do not believe that way. Did not Abraham, David, and many other men of God in the Bible have more than one woman? It is not sin."

Duncan wanted to speak for himself. "It is sin, according to the Bible. In the Old Testament, sometimes men of God took more than one wife. But this was not the perfect will of God. Today we live in New Testament times. Jesus said if we marry more than one woman, we commit adultery. I understand from this Scripture it is sin."

The clan members argued back and forth for some time. Finally, some of the old men began nodding their heads. "You have answered well," the *jaduong* replied. "We do not practice the Bible the way you do. But you are right."

Pastor William spoke again. "Now we want to leave Wilkister here. You see Duncan has not chased her rudely. We have brought her here, so that she may stay. Do you see it as good?"

The elders spoke among themselves for some time. "It is good," the spokesman finally said. "You may go, and Wilkister will stay here always. Maybe someone else will marry her," he added as an afterthought.

Duncan replied, "I am sorry for the pain I've caused Wilkister. I hope if Wilkister marries again, she does it in a good way. I hope her husband will bring cows for her even if their marriage is not legalized, so that she can be married in a way God recognizes as true marriage."

The jaduong replied, "It is good. What you have said is good. Now we release you, that you may go in peace."

Before the men left, they all stood, and the spokesman led them in a loud prayer, according to the manner of the Roho church.

As they headed back home, Duncan felt light and free compared with the heaviness he had carried on the way to Wilkister's family home. He had forgiven Alseba. And the matter of Wilkister was settled. He felt affirmed by the Spirit that he had done the right thing.

But he knew he must tell the pastor about his clash with Alseba. "Pastor," he said faintly as they drove home together.

"Yes?" asked William, turning his head a little to catch Duncan's expression.

"*Lokna wach,*" (interpret for me) he asked the interpreter. The pastor and Duncan usually communicated by mixing Luo and English, but it was easier with an interpreter. Duncan spilled the whole story—what Alseba had done with his money, how they had quarreled, and how angry he had felt.

"On the way to Katito," he continued, "God overcame my heart with conviction, and I confessed my anger to Him. That is when I truly forgave Alseba. I need to make peace with Alseba when we reach home, because I left before things were fixed between us."

The pastor replied, "I am glad if you are sorry. A Christian should treat his wife with kindness and respect. Anger can make us do many bad things we will later regret. So it's important we control our anger as you did. God will give you grace to make things right with Alseba. His power is enough to help you overcome! I'll pray for you."

"Thank you, pastor, for your prayers," Duncan replied." I need them. I want to be a Christian who gives God glory."

"That's good," Pastor William returned. "May God bless you. " By this time they had reached Duncan's home. "We'll see you tomorrow morning in instruction class," said the pastor as he squeezed Duncan's hand in farewell.

"I'll be there," promised Duncan.

When he entered his hut, Alseba was nowhere in sight. After calling her and searching fruitlessly in his maize and rice fields, he went to see Mama Dolphine.

"*Hodi*," said Duncan politely.

"*Donji,*" said Mama Dolphine. Her mouth was set in a firm, disapproving line. "Duncan, Alseba ran away to her mother." He hoped his shock didn't register in his eyes.

Mama went on, "She is thinking that you were very angry with her even if you tried to sound kind. It seems you were just cheating her that you forgave her. She is afraid you might stop being nice and beat her because of your quarrel. Since you became a Christian, you have become a different person. But Alseba still fears your temper."

Duncan was speechless. What could he tell Mama Dolphine? How would he get Alseba to come back to him?

chapter eighteen

Growth

Duncan shrugged and headed for the empty house. Slumping on a stool, he sighed deeply. *Now what? First I send one wife home, then the other one leaves too! God, where are You?* He felt very alone. Picking up his Luo Bible, he scanned the pages for direction or comfort.

When he came to Psalm 37, he found a blessing in verses one through eight. *How I wish I could have peace in my home,* his heart cried. The next verse seemed to calm his fears. "Find your joy only in the Lord, and He will give you what your heart desires," the Luo version said. Duncan realized he had been searching for his joy in the wrong places.

He knelt down by the stool and prayed in a whisper, "Oh Lord, You know I've been searching for my joy in things like making money and having the perfect family. I have depended too much on the pastor too. Please forgive me for this. I ask that You would help me to find my joy in You alone. Thank You for Your blood which sets me free!"

Cool streams of peace enveloped Duncan's heart. Although he still wasn't sure what it would take to get Alseba to return to him, he knew that with God's help, he could face anything. Besides, hadn't the Lord promised that the desires of his heart would be granted?

With a light step, he returned to Mama Dolphine's cooking fire for his evening meal.

After he ate, he sought Mama Dolphine out in the cookhouse. "Mama Dolphine, thank you for the good food. I am very satisfied. I know I have done wrong in getting angry with Alseba," he admitted. "I have confessed this sin to the Lord, and I feel at peace that He has forgiven me."

Mama lifted her head. "That is good," she said. "But what are you going to do? Being sorry will not bring Alseba back again."

Must she always be so practical? Out loud Duncan admitted, "This is true. I fear I will need to collect her at her home. The clan may not agree to let her come back since I haven't paid dowry yet." He sighed. "I don't want to ask the pastor to go on another journey with me, since he just took me to Wilkister's home. I know I depend on him too much."

Mama Dolphine nodded, her voluminous chins wobbling. "May I go with you?" She stopped and searched Duncan's face. "Can you afford even one cow?"

Duncan slumped. "No. I am having debts with various people. Me, also I'm wanting to pay back the pastor for the time I stole from the missionaries. I wish Jaduong would help a little, but I know there is no use to ask."

Mama nodded wisely. Then she shrugged. "We can only pray God and hope those clan members will let her go freely. But I think I will go alone first and see if I can persuade her to come back. The clan will not be as apt to demand something of me as they would of you."

Duncan nodded. "That is a good plan."

Mama Dolphine's gaze bored into him as the evening shadows tried to hide his face from her view. "Duncan, I was so happy when you became a Christian. I was disappointed when you became angry with Alseba. Now you will have to bear the consequences. But I want to tell you I'm very happy that you sent Wilkister home. I know you didn't say much, but I was seeing that it was difficult for you. God will bless you. You will overcome Satan!" she encouraged.

Duncan's heart thrilled to see her forgiveness and renewed confidence in him. "Thank you, Mama. I know I would not be saved if you hadn't prayed for me. You have been better to me than a real mother could have been." She smiled tenderly, and they shook hands before parting ways for the night.

Mama Dolphine left early the next morning for Alseba's home. She was gone for several days. During that time it rained so much Duncan feared his maize would be flooded. He had no time to do bike-taxi work because he needed to dig drainage ditches around his fields to save the crops. *Oh God, please give us a good harvest,* he prayed. *You know we need the money desperately.*

As he worked, Duncan agonized about Alseba. *Maybe she will not want to return.* Then he remembered how Psalm 37 had encouraged him. If I find my joy only in the Lord, He will give me my heart's desires, he reminded himself. So when the doubts came to plague his peace of mind, Duncan sang and meditated on Scripture. Often he would pray that God's will might be done in their marriage.

Several days later when Duncan headed home from the field because of impending rain, he spied the bulky figure of Mama Dolphine coming up the path. Was there someone else with her? Duncan strained to look. His pulse raced with joy. A petite lady carrying a bundle walked slowly down the path with a small child tagging behind her.

Duncan stepped inside his house to wait for them, collapsed into the one-armed chair, and began praising God in his heart. Alseba was soon inside. He shook her hand in the reserved way of his people, but his wide grin betrayed his delight. Otieno shook his hand with a resounding smack, the way Luos show their enthusiasm. Duncan smiled and took his son on his knee.

"I missed you," he admitted to Alseba. "So you gave birth while you were gone?" He pulled back the blanket to look at the tiny bundle nestled in Alseba's arms. "A girl?" he asked. "She's healthy?"

Alseba nodded. "A sister for Otieno. We can begin thinking of a name." Duncan smiled and gestured for her to sit on the stool. They exchanged many typical greetings. Then she looked at the mud floor. "Duncan, I'm sorry for taking that money. I did wrong." She seemed scared.

Duncan touched her arm. "Alseba, I really do forgive you. I also did wrong by getting angry with you like that. Please forgive me."

When Alseba looked up, teary diamonds trembled on her eyelashes. "I forgive you. I believe you are saying the truth. Now we can live in a good way," she added, as though hoping everything would be perfect from now on.

"But we need God's help," he said. "I wish you would go with me to the church. I have been going to the instruction classes, and the teaching is sweet."

But Alseba was stubborn. "No, I don't want to go. The white man's church is not for me." Duncan knew some men would force their wives to attend church with them, but he worried that this might affect the peace of their family. So he let her stay at home while he attended church every Sunday.

After a week, Duncan and Alseba decided to name their baby girl after Mama Dolphine, since Mama had been the first to inquire about a name. Besides, Duncan loved Mama Dolphine and wanted to honor her in some way. Since the baby was born in the daytime, her Luo name was Achieng.

For a while, Duncan took his bike to do taxi work while Alseba worked in the fields. Soon the rice was ripe, and then the hard work of harvesting and threshing it began. Duncan's bike stood idle during those months.

After he had milled and sold the rice, the additional workers he had hired needed to be paid. He also reimbursed the farmer whose bulls had plowed the field. When the miller's bill was paid, Duncan counted the remaining shillings in dismay.

"Alseba," he said, "We made a very small profit from our rice. I hope our maize brings us a better return."

"At least we got something," she reminded him. "Some people's fields flooded when those big rains came, and they lost everything. You can now pay back some of your debts."

"Yes, you're right," admitted Duncan. "We can be thankful for this harvest. Now you can pay the mama who owns the duka where we have been buying food on credit. I've already paid Jaduong for the goat he paid the witchdoctor to lift the curse a year ago. That will leave only two hundred shillings. I want to give that to the pastor."

"Why? So he will baptize you?"

Alseba's sarcasm made Duncan flinch. Then he replied, "No, the pastor cannot be bribed to baptize anyone. You know why I am giving him money. It's because of restitution. He isn't requiring me to pay back everything I took, but I want to give back at least some of it."

Her back rigid, Alseba pressed her lips into a thin line. Baby Dolphine cried, sensing the tension in the room. This provided a welcome diversion, and Alseba tried to calm the infant. She did not quarrel further about the matter, but Duncan still felt her strong disapproval.

After several more months, the rains tapered off, and it appeared the dry season was beginning ahead of schedule. Farmers for kilometers around feared for their maize, since the rains had stopped just as the ears were forming on the stalk.

One day, Duncan fell to his knees in the maize field. "Oh Lord," he cried aloud, "You know how much we need this maize! I still have a debt with Pius, and I want to pay the pastor at least five hundred more shillings. We need this maize to eat during the dry season, too. Please send us rain! You know how much we need it! And it's not only Alseba and I, it's also the neighbors who are needing this rain." Then Duncan checked himself. "But Lord, You know what we need more than I do. Not my will, but Your will be done."

Though ignorant of the outcome, Duncan felt safe in God's care. A peace washed over him as he shouldered his hoe and parted the maize to walk home. He met Alseba a few feet ahead. Was she listening to my prayer? he wondered. She hurried along the path, little Dolphine bobbing up and down in the cloth tied to her back.

When Alseba brought in the evening meal later that night, Duncan scanned her face for signs of what she was feeling. Somehow he felt she had heard every word of his prayer.

That night as they lay in bed, Duncan shivered when the wind crept between the roof and the wall and tried to penetrate the covers with its icy fingers. Then he heard a crack of thunder. He sprang out of bed and dashed outside. After a while, he heard a wall of rain approaching. He clapped with joy and dashed back into the house when the sheets of rain reached their hut. He heard Alseba giggling in the bedroom. "It seems God answered your prayer," she said.

So she did hear, thought Duncan. He smiled in the darkness. "God doesn't always answer my prayers with a 'yes.' But maybe He wants to strengthen my faith. Maybe He wants you to believe in Him too." Alseba gave a noncommittal grunt.

After that soaking rain, God blessed their fields with several more showers, and they were able to harvest a good crop of maize. But when Duncan paid his debt to Pius, he only had five hundred shillings left, along with one sack of maize. They had sold the rest.

Duncan worried. He sat in the field, drinking cold chai, after having chopped down the maize stalks with a machete. *God, what shall I do? Alseba will be angry if I give away the only thing we have left to live on.* Still worried, Duncan shuffled home with his machete.

chapter nineteen

A Church Member at Last

THE MORNING OF DUNCAN'S LONG-AWAITED BAPTISM DAWNED COOL and fresh, like most mornings during the broiling hot days of dry season. He had coaxed Alseba until she agreed to come to church to witness this special event.

"I'm coming today, but that doesn't mean I'm coming every Sunday," she said tartly. Duncan's eyes sparkled in spite of her gruff words. *Maybe she is softening,* he told himself. *She's trying not to admit it, but I think God is speaking to her deep inside.*

Duncan walked ahead slowly, then waited by the main road for Alseba to catch up with him. Her small figure hurried down the path, leading little Otieno by the hand and carrying baby Dolphine on her back.

When Alseba caught up with him, Duncan tried to explain the significance of baptism to her as they walked together. "You see, when I was saved, God poured out His Spirit on me. So when I am baptized is not when I will receive the Holy Spirit. He already lives in my heart." Alseba grunted. Duncan wished she'd ask some questions. When she remained silent, he simply went on.

"Baptism is a symbol of what happened to me when I was born again," he explained. "It's an outward ceremony with a spiritual meaning."

Alseba appeared bored. She studied the beautifully weeded field of maize they were passing and commented that the owners must have planted earlier than Duncan. He sighed. Was it any use trying to talk to her about spiritual things?

Thinking about the maize field made him wonder what Alseba would say if she knew he planned to use the five hundred shillings from their last harvest to repay the pastor. *I'll have to tell her soon.* He straightened his shoulders suddenly. *I won't let the cares of money disturb my happiness today.*

After a while, Duncan took Otieno in his strong arms and carried him, since the two-year-old could not walk so far. Duncan looked across the road and saw a neighbor striding down the path. They waved to each other. The man's wife struggled quite a ways behind him, with her infant tied to her back, her basket balanced on her head, and her toddler cradled in her arms. Although most other Luos let their wives carry everything in this way, Duncan tried to help his wife with the load. Since he had been saved, the Holy Spirit prompted him to do thoughtful things for Alseba that had never occurred to him before.

Mama Dolphine lagged some distance behind her son and his family, too old and heavy to keep up with them. Duncan would normally have matched his pace to hers, but his excitement made him walk *chap chap.* (quickly) Today he would join the visible body of Christ. He didn't want to be late for his own baptism!

Three of the other five applicants for baptism were already at church. They spoke with each other in the yard since it was still too early for the service to begin.

"My, how different those ladies look with a cape dress and white veil!" Alseba marveled. Duncan agreed.

He and his family entered the church reverently. Alseba took a seat next to Mama Dolphine. She craned her neck to watch Duncan walk up and sit on the front bench with the other baptismal applicants.

When it was Duncan's turn to give his testimony, he faced the congregation confidently and said, "I greet all of you, praise Jesus."

In unison, the congregation replied, "Praise the Lord."

Duncan spoke clearly through an interpreter. "I used to be a very sinful man, but Jesus saved me. In the past, I was involved in things like stealing, fornication, and polygamy. Praise the Lord!"

"Amen!" the congregation chorused. This was the typical way of keeping the people's attention. Duncan went on. "I was a very sinful man. But Jesus took me and washed me with His blood. Because of this, I have a changed life. I ask all of you to pray for me so I may remain faithful. Satan often attacks me, but I want to continue to be a follower of Jesus."

He noticed Alseba's eyes were fixed on him. *I wonder if she has noticed the change in me,* Duncan thought. *How I long for her to find Jesus too.*

Before the ceremony, all the applicants were asked a series of questions. Duncan's heart sang as he promised to be committed to Christ till death. He remembered the Scripture in which Jesus said, "If you know these things, you are happy if you do them." *So this is the joy He spoke of,* Duncan mused.

Then the bishop scooped up water from a basin with his hands and poured it on Duncan's head three times as he said, "I baptize you with water in the name of the Father, the Son, and the Holy Spirit." Duncan waited with head bowed as the bishop baptized the other applicants.

Then the bishop said, "Duncan, in the name of Christ and His church, I give you my hand. Arise." The bishop helped him to his feet. "And as you have been buried by baptism in the likeness of His death, even so you shall walk in newness of life. I welcome you as a part of the body of Christ and a member of this church." Chills went up and down Duncan's spine.

He sat back down on the bench. Already he was looking forward to Holy Communion in a couple months. As a church member, he would qualify to partake if he had examined himself and his life was pure before God and the rest of the congregation.

On the way home, Otieno whimpered, "*Adenyo!*" (I'm hungry)

Duncan picked him up. "Sorry," he sympathized. "Mama will cook *ugali* when we reach home." Duncan and Alseba had stayed quite a while after the service. The other members wanted a chance to welcome the baptismal class into the church. Many of them had shared a word of encouragement with Duncan, and some friends wanted to meet his wife.

As Duncan and Alseba walked home, he whispered, "Alseba, do you want to be a Christian too? Do you want Jesus to change your life?"

"I'm a good person," Alseba retorted. "I don't need to have my life changed."

But Duncan could tell this was a cover-up; she really didn't feel that content with herself. However, he didn't want to quarrel with her, so he simply held his peace. As he walked, he breathed another prayer for her salvation.

When they reached the dala, Alseba and Mama Dolphine cooked the noon meal together. Duncan, sitting on the mud ledge of the house, could easily hear their conversation through the open window.

Alseba asked her mother-in-law, "I have been seeing how the ladies in your church wear a uniform and tie a white veil. Many other churches do that too. Why does your church ask the members to dress like this all the time? Other churches wear their uniform only to church."

Mama Dolphine replied, "I don't know. I just do it because it is a church rule. Maybe Duncan knows."

Duncan stretched and yawned. He stepped into the cookhouse and said, "Mama Dolphine, you really should know why you dress the way you do. It's not just a church rule." Alseba looked up at him, her eyes wide with curiosity.

I'm glad she's interested. Duncan was pleased to explain, "The Bible teaches us to be separate from unsaved people, who don't wear modest clothing. We don't want clothes that are revealing, so that's why we adopted this pattern. We want to be modest all the time, not only on Sundays. Are you getting me?"

Alseba and Mama Dolphine murmured, "*Eee.*"

"The sisters tie the veil all the time to show they are submitting their husbands and to God. However, women are not worth less than men, as most Luos think. We are of equal importance and value. The man needs to submit to Christ's authority. The woman, in turn, submits to the man. Our sisters all wear the same type of veil because it is a specific symbol. It's more than a dust protection like many mamas wear." That was quite a mouthful.

Had they really understood?

Alseba didn't have any more questions, and Mama Dolphine nodded. "You've answered well," she said. Duncan went back out to sit on the ledge and sighed. *Is Alseba interested in becoming one of us? Will my prayers ever be answered?*

After several months, the church reorganized their responsibilities. Duncan was chosen to be an usher for the next six months.

"I'm glad I can be an usher," he confided in Alseba, "But it's hard work. Washington and I are in charge of passing out and collecting the songbooks and keeping the attendance record."

"You mean you collect the songbooks after the church is done singing?" asked Alseba.

"Yes," he replied. "We count them every Sunday to be sure no one had slipped one into their basket. People often take them home to use there, but it is not allowed." Alseba's eyes betrayed her surprise.

"Now and then, Washington has to chase the children, who pick lemons off the nearby tree, back into the church. But I'd rather count the offering money. I do it at a little table in front of the church."

"That way no one can accuse you of stealing?" asked Alseba.

He nodded. "Washington has to be careful to keep the children inside because they like to use stones to scratch names in the paint of the pastor's vehicle." Alseba stifled a giggle.

"Washington needs to act a little like a policeman. Sometimes he even pokes the old mamas who sleep in church."

This time Alseba laughed aloud. "Don't people despise him?" she wondered.

"No. Everyone loves Washington. He's just doing his job. He has a nice way with people, even the ones he is correcting." Alseba nodded, seemingly impressed.

The next Sunday, Washington asked Duncan to be in charge of the attendance record for the members. He sat at the entrance of the church very early and put an X beside the name of every member who came in on time.

If they were late, they were marked accordingly. Sometimes the pastor hung the attendance record on the bulletin board to encourage prompt attendance. *This church does things very differently from other churches, but the attendance record is a good idea,* Duncan thought. He wondered if Alseba would smile about this.

One day, Pastor William's wife talked to Duncan. "Your wife is not a church member. Is she saved?"

Duncan replied, "No, she is not. I pray for her daily."

"Do you think she would be interested in some Bible teaching if I came to visit her every week?"

Duncan hesitated for one long moment. "I think she would be happy if you would visit her weekly. It is good if you can bring her the Word of God. I hope she can be saved in this way. Yes, this is a very good plan. When will you come?"

The pastor's wife thought a little. "How would it work if I came every Thursday?"

"That is a good plan," Duncan agreed. They shook hands Luo style, then Duncan hurried home. Did God have it planned that the pastor's wife would have Bible studies with Alseba for a purpose? Would this be the means of Alseba's salvation?

chapter twenty

A New Vision

Duncan parked his bike beside the mud hut. He winced as he remembered, *Today I need to tell Alseba I gave that money to the pastor.* He removed his bill cap and entered the house. Seeing Otieno sitting on a reed mat playing with baby Dolphine, he caught up his little daughter and asked Otieno, "Where is Mother?"

"She went to the duka," the three-year-old replied. Duncan knew she would be back soon since she had left the children alone.

Before too long, Alseba was at the door with a small bag containing cooking oil and *sakumu*. A basket of freshly ground maize was on her head. Since Duncan had torn down the cookhouse after Wilkister left, Alseba cooked in the main house or outside over three stones. She often grumbled about it, but Duncan insisted this was a good way to show the neighbors he had left polygamy.

Duncan meandered over to her as she was lighting her cooking fire for the evening meal. "How was the day?" he asked.

"Fine," Alseba replied. When the fire was blazing, she poked several more sticks under the pot and added water. After sprinkling in a handful of cornmeal, she turned to her husband and gestured for him to be seated on a low stool. He sat there, fidgeting, unsure how to begin.

"What is it?" she asked after several minutes of silence. Evidently she realized Duncan wanted to tell her something.

He sighed. There would be no easy way to say it. "You know very well I am not earning much money with my job as bike taxi. But at least we are getting enough to eat. We are still using that sack of maize from our last harvest, but it will soon be finished." He paused.

"What about that five hundred shillings we got from selling our grain?" Alseba reminded him. She cut up *sakumu* as fast as her knife could slice.

"Do you remember my plan?" Duncan asked. He watched her back become rigid. Apparently she had not forgotten. "I wanted to make restitution to the missionary for the money I had stolen. He isn't asking me to pay back all the money--just enough to show I'm truly sorry."

Alseba snipped even faster. Her eyes glared. "I do not understand your ways. If you are sorry and the missionary has forgiven you, why do you repay him that money? Even you have told me he is not requiring you to pay anything. *Odiero* (wealthy white man) does not need our precious income. Just leave this word of restitution. You are not forced to pay the man." She grabbed another cluster of *sakumu* and snapped off the stems.

"Alseba." Duncan stopped her with a hand on her arm. "Suppose someone stole from you the sum of one thousand shillings. If he was sorry, would you believe him if he repaid you nothing?" Alseba stopped cutting for a moment as she pondered his question. "Suppose he was poor?" Duncan went on. "Would you not believe he was sorry if he gave back two hundred shillings? Even so, I need to show my change in heart. The Bible teaches we should do restitution. Are you getting me?"

"Yes," she replied, then pressed her mouth into the familiar straight line. He could tell she was still upset but would say nothing more about it. *I wish she would agree with me! I wish she were one with me in my walk with the Lord!* He realized now was not the time to tell her about the pastor's wife's desire to bring her the Word of God.

The following Sunday, Duncan and several other brothers visited Washington after church. The men sat in the living room, visiting together while Washington's wife prepared the food. "There are so many people dying of AIDS," Washington remarked. The other men agreed.

"This means there are a lot of orphans," observed Duncan. They all knew this was true. Nobody knew who all was HIV positive, but Duncan suspected many of the widows in church carried the virus. Most of the orphans who came for Sunday school had lost their parents to the scourge of AIDS. Duncan keenly remembered his own experience as an orphan—first on the streets and then in an orphanage. Who would care for the orphans in the church?

"I wish our church could build an orphanage," remarked one of the other brothers.

"Why don't they?" someone else wondered.

Duncan spoke up hesitantly. "I think the church brothers should do without help from the white people. If nationals were in charge, we could go on with the project even if the missionaries had to leave."

The brethren looked surprised. Silence reigned as they pondered this suggestion. "How could we do this without funds from America?" Washington wondered. "How could we afford a building?"

Duncan remembered Mama June's orphanage, which was supported by foreign donors. Later the money flow was cut off, and she was forced to close down. "We have widows," he suggested. "Perhaps we could place destitute orphans in the homes of these widows so the children might receive good care. They have both lost their loved ones. Maybe they could both find comfort in belonging to someone again."

The others clapped. "That's a wonderful plan!" They all began talking at once.

Washington looked troubled. "But we still need money for school fees, food, and clothes," he said. "I'm sure we could find sponsors in America."

"I think you're right," Duncan finally agreed. "Maybe we should ask the pastor." The others felt this was a good idea.

Duncan was deep in thought as he pedalled home, and prayed as he drove along.

When Duncan reached home, Mama Dolphine, who was caring for Otieno, told him Alseba had gone to the field to weed the maize. It had sprouted beautifully since rainy season had come with its daily showers. *She knows I don't like for her to work on Sunday,* he thought rather grumpily.

Duncan trotted out to the field and found her working, with little Dolphine tied on her back. The baby girl was sleeping and bobbed along as her mother worked. "Come here," he called to Alseba as he drew near. He gestured to the shade of a blue gum tree.

Alseba walked over and plopped down beside him. "Such hard work when the sun is shining so brightly!" she exclaimed.

Duncan decided not to remind her she should have simply left the work for a weekday. He wanted her in an amiable mood for the news he was going to tell her. "Alseba, I have a good word for you," he began. "The pastor's wife, Nina, wants to come visit you on Thursday. Do you accept?"

Alseba's pretty face broke into a smile. "I accept. That is a good thing! I only met her once. But I like visitors."

Duncan twirled a little twig around and around in his fingers. "Alseba, the pastor's wife wants to teach you the Word of God. She wants to come every week. Can you accept?" He stole a glance to check her face, but could read nothing in her deadpan expression.

After several long moments, she asked, "Have you given her leave to come?"

"Yes, I have." Duncan could not deny it. "But I will send her word at the midweek Bible study if you are too busy."

Alseba rose abruptly. "Ah, it is not bad," she said, grabbing her hoe. "I am not saying I want to be saved or join your church, but it is good if the pastor's wife wants to give me teaching." Alseba shouldered her hoe and headed back for the maize field.

"Alseba, come home with me," Duncan pled with her retreating back. "You do not need to work on Sunday."

She swung around to face him. "The weeds grow on Sunday same as they do on weekdays. The one who does not work does not eat," she flung at him.

Duncan flinched. Was she implying that he was lazy? Rather than retaliating with bitter words, he decided to be quiet. He headed to the house alone. *How can I win Alseba to the Lord?*

Duncan headed for the shade of the mango tree where Jaduong was dozing in a chair. Duncan stretched out on his back and looked into the sky. *Oh God,* he prayed. *I have so many cares. There's my family to feed. My wife is unsaved, and I feel so alone in my walk with You.* Duncan sighed. *But I know You will help me. Please win Alseba to You. It is not in my power, but I know You are the Almighty One.*

Duncan's thoughts drifted to the new idea they had talked about at Washington's house. He worried about how they would find the funding for the project. Like a flash, the thought came to him: *If you need sponsors from America, God will provide them.* A great peace and comfort stole over him.

Soon the evening shadows lengthened. Alseba and baby Dolphine returned from the maize field. Duncan got up from his spot in the shade and offered to put the hoe away for his wife. He took the baby so she could prepare supper. *Will Alseba ever catch on that I am different because of Christ coming into my life? How much longer will she hold onto her stubbornness?*

chapter twenty-one

Sickness

THE PASTOR'S WIFE, NINA, BEGAN TO VISIT ALSEBA WEEKLY. THEIR friendship developed as the two studied Bible lessons, helped each other cook, and even worked together in the fields.

One Sunday morning as Duncan was about to leave for church, Alseba emerged from their house in her best clothes. She announced that she wanted to begin attending church with Duncan.

"Are you sure?" he asked in surprise, then wished he hadn't. *I don't want to give her a chance to back down.*

"Yes," Alseba replied. She laughed at his amazement. "I thought you had schemed for this all along in arranging for Bible studies with the pastor's wife. The Bible lessons persuaded me I need Jesus to change my life. Not only that, but you are a very different man since you became a Christian. This spoke to me most of all. I wish to be saved and join the church."

"Is this true? Praise the Lord!" Duncan wanted to do a cartwheel, but he was holding baby Dolphine. He let his love for Alseba shine through his eyes. "I was discouraged, and had almost given up hope that you would ever want to be saved. But I see God was speaking to you all along. He hadn't given up on you. I'm very happy!" Duncan walked to church as if on a cloud.

After the service, Alseba asked to meet with the pastor's wife and another sister. "I want to be saved," she told them. Duncan listened outside the church window as the two sisters led his wife to Christ. Excitement pulsed through his veins. *This is actually happening. I can't believe it!*

The pastor's wife, Nina, asked her interpreter to read many Scriptures in Luo. "The Bible says everyone is born a sinner. Do you believe you are a sinner?" she asked Alseba.

"Yes, I have done many wrong things," Duncan heard Alseba admit. She understood the plan of salvation perfectly as they explained it to her, for those Bible studies were not without fruit.

Alseba prayed with Nina and her interpreter. She confessed her sins to God and asked for the blood of Jesus to cleanse her. Duncan felt goose bumps rising as he listened.

Soon Alseba emerged from the prayer room with a radiant smile. They walked home from church together. "I am going to be on the waiting list to enter instruction class for three Sundays," Alseba said. "If I don't miss a service, the pastor will do an interview for me. Then I can be in instruction class. The pastor's wife said I can be baptized after I get enough lessons from the instruction book."

That's very good," Duncan said with a grin. "I have waited for this day for so long. I'm very happy! You have no idea how many prayers I said for you."

"Thank you," Alseba said softly. "I'm thinking that's why God didn't give up on me."

After dusk fell, Duncan suggested they sit down together for evening prayers for the first time. How long Duncan had waited for this! Together they sang Duncan's favorite hymn, "There Is Power in the Blood." A smoking wick from a tin-can lantern flickered, but the light of Jesus flooded their faces with a greater radiance. Next, Duncan read Psalm 37, since this portion of Scripture had blessed him in days gone by. He closed with prayer. Alseba was still too shy to pray in front of him, but he was sure she would eventually pray aloud in family worship.

As Duncan lay in bed that night listening to Alseba's even breathing, he prayed, *My heart is full of thanksgiving to You, O God. It's so wonderful to have a totally Christian home now that Alseba is also saved. Thank You, God, for answering my prayer.*

One day Duncan weeded the maize alone while Alseba stayed at home because Otieno was sick. When the sun was high in the sky, Alseba came running out to the field. He took one look at her worried face and knew something was wrong.

"Duncan, Otieno is sick *ahinya*." (very much) She drew out the ahinya for emphasis. "Do we have money to take him to the doctor? He just vomits everything he drinks and is very hot."

Duncan's brow puckered. Did his son have cholera? "I don't have much money, but I'll take him on the bicycle and see what they can do for him at Ahero Health Center."

Alseba looked relieved. She trotted back to the house with Duncan close behind. When Duncan looked at the three-year-old and felt his son's forehead, he was alarmed. *I wish we had decided to take him in sooner.*

They left Baby Dolphine with Duncan's mother. His wife perched on the back of his bike while he held it steady for her. Then Mama Dolphine handed the feverish Otieno to Alseba.

Duncan had never pedaled so fast. When he arrived at the clinic, his spirits drooped as he saw the long line waiting to be treated. Just before sundown, they were finally permitted to see the physician.

The small, poorly equipped health center had a few beds for patients who needed to stay. Duncan wrinkled his nose at the rank smell of ointment mingled with vomit. The doctor admitted Otieno and ordered IVs because the child was so dehydrated. Alseba spread a thin cloth on the bare mattress. She hadn't thought to bring a blanket.

"I'll stay here with Otieno overnight," Alseba volunteered. "You need to be feeling well to work tomorrow. We will need money to buy things like syringes, IVs, and medicine."

"*Aaya*," Duncan told her. "I'll bring to you whatever I earn tomorrow."

"Bring some blankets and food," Alseba reminded him. "Oh, I'm so afraid. What will happen to Otieno? Do you think someone put a curse on us?"

The two pairs of worried eyes met. "No, I don't think so," Duncan replied. "If we are saved, a curse cannot touch us." Alseba smiled briefly, but the worried look would not leave her eyes. Their son was desperately ill. They shook hands in the customary Luo good-bye, then Duncan biked home.

That evening, Duncan returned to the hospital and to give Alseba the money he had earned and the other items she had requested. "They did some tests," Alseba soberly informed Duncan. "Otieno has typhoid."

"Typhoid! That's serious." Duncan's stomach churned. His face mirrored Alseba's distress. "Let's pray," he suggested. Together they bowed their heads. "Oh Lord, please look down and have mercy on our son. If You agree, heal him. Give us grace for this difficult time." Together they said, "Amen."

Duncan biked home as dusk was falling. But when he went to bed, he couldn't sleep. *Oh Lord, please heal my child,* he pled. *Don't let him die from this terrible fever.* He tossed and turned. *God, I don't have enough money for him to stay in the hospital for a long time. What am I going to do?* Then he remembered the alms committee gave a hundred shillings to any church member who had medical needs. Although this would barely touch the bill he would receive, it would help a little.

The next morning, Duncan biked to Kobura to ask the alms committee member from his district for some money. "My son is very sick with typhoid, and he may need to stay at the clinic in Ahero for a while."

The old man shook his head sadly. "I'm sorry. This is near the end of the month, and all the money is finished. Next month we will get more money. I wish I had something to give."

"I don't know what I'm going to do," said Duncan in desperation. "Surely God will help me."

The elderly man's face filled with compassion. "Even though there is nothing in the needs fund, I will give you something myself. I hope it can help you a bit." He reached in his pocket and pulled out one hundred shillings.

Duncan's eyes glistened with unexpected moisture. "Thank you! May God bless you." He knew this man was unemployed and also had a family to support. "Thank you so much," Duncan repeated as he gave the man a fervent handshake before he left. Ashamed, he chided himself for his lack of faith.

That evening, Duncan again went to visit Alseba and Otieno at the clinic. He smiled as he told Alseba of the loving gift from this brother. "At least we have one bright spot in this trial."

Duncan gave a start as he noticed the hollow spots under Alseba's eyes from staying up nights with their ill son. "Otieno is still very sick," she told him. "I think he's getting worse. He doesn't even talk."

"Don't be discouraged," Duncan told her tenderly, trying to be strong for her sake. "Being a Christian means we have many trials to test our faith. Stay true to God." Duncan's words sounded good, but didn't want to admit his own discouragement, even to himself.

Otieno needed to stay at the Health Center for an entire week. Duncan tried his best to pay for the syringes, medicines, and hospital fees. But he soon used up all his money. Sometimes the family went to bed hungry so Otieno could remain in the ward. Eventually the clinic needed to release Otieno, who was still quite ill, because Duncan simply could no longer pay the fees. He was left with a debt of five hundred shillings.

Lord what am I going to do? Duncan cried out as he sat under the mango tree one evening. *My son is still sick, and I'm barely making enough to feed my family. The money in the alms fund is finished so I can't get help there. Please work a miracle and heal my son.* Duncan had never felt such despair. Where was God?

The next day Otieno grew even worse. In desperation, Duncan biked to a pay phone in Ahero and called the pastor collect. "Pastor William," he said. "My son is very sick with typhoid fever. He was admitted to Ahero Health Center for a week, but they had to release him because I ran out of money. The alms fund is finished too. I don't know what to do. I'm afraid my son will die." He couldn't hide the tremor in his voice.

"I'm sorry, Duncan," comforted the pastor. "I knew your son was sick, but I didn't realize it was so serious. I'll come over right away and see what I can do. You can expect me in half an hour." Duncan breathed a sigh of relief.

After what seemed like hours, the welcome purr of the pastor's vehicle reached the ears of Duncan and Alseba. Duncan invited Pastor William, and his wife into the house. After the pastor had led the group in a fervent prayer, he and his wife went to the bedroom to see the child. "He is very sick, don't you think?" the pastor asked with concern.

"Yes," the pastor's wife agreed. "Hadn't you better take him to the hospital?"

They all agreed the situation was serious. Pastor William decided to transport Alseba and Otieno to the Russia Hospital immediately. Alseba climbed into the vehicle, and Duncan handed Otieno up to her. Pastor William assured Duncan, "I'll pay for the bill at Russia Hospital—don't worry about that."

"Thank you." Duncan's face relaxed into a smile as relief flooded over him. "May God reward you." Yet they left Duncan with this unspoken worry. *Will we be able to get help for our son soon enough? Will he live?*

chapter twenty-two

The Grim Reaper

Heavy hearted, Duncan strapped his Bible to the back of his bike before he began cycling to the Wednesday Bible study. It had been two days since Pastor William had taken Alseba and their sick son to the Russian Hospital. *I wonder how Otieno is feeling. Is he getting better? Or--God forbid--is he dying?*

Duncan's church had Bible study every Wednesday. Today a brother from Boya, Alseba's home area, had volunteered to host the meeting.

"Welcome!" He greeted the brothers with the holy kiss and ushered them inside. Since the hut was so tiny, the women sat on reed mats outside. They could still hear the preaching through the mud walls.

Instead of entering the hut, Duncan beckoned for Pastor William to come talk with him in private. His burning question was, "Pastor, how is my son?"

The pastor soberly replied, "He is not doing very well. I'm afraid he cannot live much longer. I think you should ride back with me to the hospital if you want to see your son alive. I'm very sorry to tell you this."

Duncan flinched and covered his face with his hands. Abruptly he walked away, leaving the pastor to enter the hut alone. *God, where are You?* he cried in his heart. *Don't You know that my son is dying? Why didn't you heal him? Why don't you do a miracle even now? I don't understand!*

Duncan's own words to Alseba came back to remind him, "When we are Christians, some trials must come to us." But God, this is too much!

Though Duncan finally shuffled into the hut where they were having Bible study, he got very little out of it. Worries robbed him of his peace of mind. Afterwards, the men and women were served a snack in their respective places. Duncan was too upset to eat, so he walked a few meters away from the hut. Staring into the distance without seeing anything, he felt numb with the pastor's news. *My son could die tonight!* The thought was too painful to bear. *And I have no money.*

Duncan saw Pastor William coming his way and wanted only to be left alone. But the pastor sympathetically put his arm around Duncan and bowed his head. At a time like this, words were not necessary. They wept together, and Duncan felt some of the tension disappear. At least Pastor William cared, and through this simple loving gesture, he had shown God's love to Duncan.

On the way to the hospital, Duncan's load of despair lifted even more, though he didn't know how much longer his son would live. *Lord, I give the situation into your hands,* he prayed. Trusting God gave peace the freedom to sweep over his rumpled spirit.

When Pastor William and Duncan reached the hospital, they headed right for the children's ward. Many nauseating smells rose up to meet them. The odor was so thick Duncan didn't want to breathe. As they drew closer, the sound of wailing reached his ears. *Someone has died,* the thought registered in his mind.

When Duncan and the pastor entered Otieno's ward, Duncan's heart stopped. Alseba was wailing loudly, bent over double. Tears streamed down her cheeks. A sheet was pulled over a small, still form on the bed. *Otieno has died.* The truth struck Duncan and almost stunned him. He wanted to deny it, but the facts remained in the cold, dark lines of Otieno's lifeless form.

Duncan walked over to Alseba and took her hand. She stopped wailing long enough to tell them in a choked voice, "He passed away one hour ago." She was obviously very broken up. Duncan swallowed hard. Had God let him down?

He lifted the sheet from his son's face, sat beside his wife, and buried his head in his hands. He tried not to cry; after all, he was a man and should be strong. Pastor William prayed for the grieving couple, but Duncan didn't hear a word he said. His bottled-up grief wanted to choke him.

With his head still in his hands, tears finally seeping from his eyes, he prayed, *God, are you there, really? Pastor William said if I draw near to you, You promised to draw near to me. Please help me not to become bitter. Help me to see your love.*

He wiped his tears, then went with the pastor to talk to the hospital officials. Duncan didn't want Otieno's body to be placed in the morgue because it was too expensive. The pastor worked for a long time to get through the process of getting a signed release and paying the bills. After receiving permission to take the body home immediately, they wrapped it in a cloth and carried it out to the Cruiser. "I will buy a coffin tomorrow morning," the pastor promised Duncan.

"Can we have the funeral tomorrow afternoon?" asked Duncan. "It is our custom to bury a child the next day. We normally do not embalm a child's body, and it will not keep for very long in this heat. Usually a child's funeral is in the morning, but we need some time to prepare things."

The pastor nodded. "Will you speak to the alms committee members about digging the grave?" he asked. Duncan agreed.

Alseba sobbed softly all the way home, holding the lifeless form. Duncan clamped his mouth shut in an attempt to be strong, but twice he had to wipe away tears from his eyes. It was a sad, silent journey. The pastor did not try to say anything, but Duncan could tell he was praying.

When they reached home, Pastor William told them, "I don't have any words to tell you how sorry I am. We are praying for you." His voice choked. By his tears, he gave better comfort than anything he could've said. The pastor drove away into the dark night, leaving a very sad family behind.

Though it was dark, Duncan biked around to tell each alms committee member about the funeral. "Will you help dig the grave tomorrow morning?" he asked them. "Also inform the members of our church."

"Yes, we'll do that," the men assured him. "We are very sorry to hear of the death," they said sympathetically.

"Thank you," said Duncan, swallowing the lump in his throat. They understood because they had also buried many close family members. People all around them were dying like flies. It made Duncan wonder sometimes if he would be next.

It was a small funeral the next afternoon, but some of Duncan's church friends were there to show their support. Duncan, Alseba, and Mama Dolphine all shared their happy memories of little Otieno. When Alseba spoke lovingly of her son, Duncan realized how healing this was for her. But at the end of her speech, she broke down. Unable to continue because of tears, she sat down. Duncan was rather uncomfortable because of her display of grief. *She should be more submissive to God's plan,* he thought to himself.

Pastor William preached a touching message, picturing three-year-old Otieno safe in Jesus' arms. He also warned those who might not be ready to enter heaven of their impending doom. The message was a great comfort to Duncan.

Still he struggled to deal with the raging emotions within him. *What a big satan this is,* he thought more than once. *I don't understand why God didn't prevent this from happening to me.*

After the message, the pastor had special prayer for Duncan's extended family. Next, an offering was lifted. Duncan and Alseba would have visitors for a while--mostly Alseba's relatives, who would need to be fed. This offering helped with food costs and other funeral expenses.

When they stood around the hole and the coffin was lowered to the ground, Alseba suddenly burst into a loud wail. She began stumbling blindly through the crowd, bumping into people as she yelled, "Woo-loo-loo-loo!" Her tears dripped off her face. She bent double, her grief and misery apparent to all. *Usually people do not wail for a child,* thought Duncan.

Dry-eyed, Duncan listened to her cries as the pastor read the usual Scripture. When he read, "Dust to dust," pastor William dropped a clod of dirt onto the coffin. He invited family members to add some dirt if they wanted to. Duncan and Mama Dolphine threw in handfuls of soil.

The church members sang solemnly as strong young men took turns shovelling dirt onto the grave. When it was all over, the funeral guests went to neighboring dalas for lunch.

In the following days, both Duncan and Alseba felt numb with grief. In a way, it was nice to have their relatives around, for it kept their minds off themselves. And yet they were a burden to feed. It also meant there were always people around. When Duncan wanted to be alone, he'd go to the field and pray.

God, I want to draw nearer to you, he'd say. *Please help us bear our load of grief. I don' t know how we'll get through the days ahead without your help. We need you.*

At the end of the day, Duncan took his Bible and read about the resurrection of Lazarus. He found a verse that said Jesus wept. *So it's all right to cry,* he realized. *Alseba has been handling her grief better than me, wailing and all. She lets herself feel the pain. I've been trying to bottle it up, pretending to be strong by not letting myself cry.*

Oh Lord, I'm sorry, he prayed. *I didn't accept Otieno's death nor allow my heart to feel its sorrow. I was bitter about the death--it seemed like you were cheating me by letting my first-born son die. I want to believe that you did the best thing by taking him to glory, as Pastor William preached at the funeral. But it's so hard, Lord!*

Then Duncan gave way to weeping. All the pent-up emotions of the past weeks let themselves loose as he shook with sobs. After his tears were spent, he returned to a house full of people with a peaceful heart. He tried to make it through each day by God's help.

There were many more times when he had to cry--even in front of other people--much to his embarrassment. Yet he found a release for his emotions in this way. He somehow tried to make it through the following weeks and months. What else was there to do?

chapter twenty-three

Under the Mango Tree

S EVERAL MONTHS LATER, PASTOR WILLIAM ASKED TO SPEAK TO DUNCAN after Bible study. Alseba and the other ladies were still drinking chai and eating sweet potatoes.

"Duncan," said the pastor kindly, "I know you've had problems with not having enough money."

"Yes." Duncan's shoulders slumped. "Bike taxi work is slow nowadays."

"I have an idea," William smiled. "We could use a man at our mission compound to do lawn work and wash vehicles. If you come once or twice a week, I could give you a job." Duncan perked up.

"How much is the pay?" he wondered.

"We could give you two hundred shillings a day. Does that sound good?"

"Yes. That is very good!" Duncan straightened his shoulders. "Alseba will be very happy." He smiled with relief.

"I'm just glad if I can help you," assured the pastor, clasping his hand tightly.

Bike taxi work never pays two hundred shillings a day. Sometimes I only make fifty. Duncan thought about his new job. *This money will help us get out of debt. Maybe I can even buy some clothes for Alseba and the baby.*

On the way home from Bible study with Alseba on the back of his bike, Duncan excitedly told her about the job offer he had from the pastor. "He will pay me two hundred shillings for working once or twice a week!"

Duncan heard Alseba's smile in her voice. "That's top wage. It seems he wants to help you."

"Yes, that's what he said. I want to buy some clothes for you and baby Dolphine. You do need clothes."

"Yes," Alseba admitted. "But I don't need more than one new dress, because I hope to be given cape dresses after I'm baptised. I only have five dresses, and two of them are in shreds. I would like a free-size dress though, since I'm expecting a child. "

"Oh, that's wonderful! I'll buy you a 'free dress.' See how God is meeting our needs! It seems He is nearer now than he was during Otieno's death," Duncan remarked.

"But He was just as close to us then as he is now." Alseba reminded him.

"That's right," admitted Duncan. "It just didn't feel like it."

"The pastor's wife says we can't always depend on our feelings," Alseba said. "When we prayed and drew near to God, He was there with us, even when we felt so sad." He was often astounded with her spiritual knowledge.

"That is true," Duncan replied. They had arrived at home, so Duncan held the bike steady for Alseba to alight.

Both of them saw it at the same time. Under Jaduong's favorite mango tree lay the emaciated form of a woman. Duncan walked closer to see who it might be. Hollow eyes stared up at him from a skeleton form. *No! It's not-- but yes! It's Wilkister.* Duncan's heart sank to the soles of his flip-flip sandals. He looked at Alseba's stunned face. As if in a daze, Duncan walked over to the sickly woman and shook her hand. She had the obvious signs of AIDS. Quickly he walked back to his house.

He looked over his shoulder and saw Alseba talking to Wilkister, but he decided he didn't want to have anything more to do with his former second wife. Not if she had AIDS! Duncan had to wonder if she had passed on the virus to him as well. The thought was too dreadful even to consider.

When he looked out the window, he saw Alseba walking slowly with Wilkister to Mama Dolphine's hut, supporting the sick woman with one arm.

Later Alseba came inside to Duncan and said, "Wilkister is very ill. She said this sickness has been going on for a few years. She has come home to die." She wrinkled up her nose as though this were not to her liking.

Duncan's temper flared. "This is not her home. I want her to leave right away. In God's sight I am not really her husband. What does she mean by coming back to us when she seems to be sick with AIDS?"

Alseba's eyes widened. "Yes, she probably has AIDS," she admitted slowly. "Wilkister's parents have rejected her and told her to go to her own home where she can be buried when she dies. According to our culture, this is her home."

"Alseba, I don't want her here!" Duncan stressed. "What can we do?"

"Are you afraid that seeing her dying of AIDS will remind you she could've passed on the virus to us as well?" Alseba wondered.

Duncan hung his head. How did she know him so well?

Alseba went on, "To say the truth, I can't say I want to have her here either. It makes me jealous because it reminds me of how you took another woman."

"Then why not send her away so we don't have to remember those things?" asked Duncan shortly.

"Well, she can't eat *ugali* anymore, but someone should cook her some *nyuka*. Can't she stay with Mama Dolphine until she dies? She can't walk anywhere far, but Mama Dolphine and I can care for her. Her days are numbered. I somehow feel sorry for her even if it brings back bad memories."

Duncan sighed. He felt no pity, only distaste. *Lord, I don't want to help Wilkister. She has never been anything but a burden to me. What shall I do?*

Then a verse came to his mind, "If your enemy hunger, feed him. If he thirsts, give him a drink. For in so doing, you shall heap coals of fire on his head, and the Lord will reward you." Duncan tried to ignore the verse.

"Alseba," he tried one last time. "Isn't there any way to send Wilkister away? Couldn't we ask the pastor to take her to her home?"

Alseba sighed. "You remember she said her family chased her away. I don't want her around any more than you do. But I feel we have a duty to care for her."

Just then, the verse about treating one's enemy well came back to Duncan's mind in a piercing flash of insight. He knew he had to listen to the Holy Spirit. "Okay," he gave in at last. "If Mama Dolphine agrees, Wilkister can stay with her. However, I will never go to see her. I have turned my back on that part of my life. Yet since I will be earning a little more money, I can provide maize for her *nyuka* as well as milk and sugar for her chai. This is not really what I want to do, but it is our duty," he said. "Why don't you go tell Wilkister? I don't even want to talk to her." *And I don't want anything more to do with her,* he told himself, feeling sick because he realized she had AIDS.

Alseba didn't look like she relished talking to Wilkister any more than Duncan did. Yet she obediently walked over to the mango tree. Duncan looked out the doorway and saw that Mama Dolphine was already with Wilkister. How thin his former wife was! How hollow her eyes! *What if she transmitted the HIV virus to me?* he thought again with a jolt. *I could have full-blown AIDS before many years just like Wilkister!* Duncan's stomach churned with worry.

When Alseba came back from making arrangments with Mama Dolphine, Duncan shared his troubles with his wife. "Both of us could have HIV," he informed her seriously. "We cannot deny that Wilkister has that disease."

Alseba's wide white eyes contrasted with her black face. "Should we get tested?" she wondered.

"Do we really want to know the diagnosis?" Duncan hedged. "That would be our death sentence."

Alseba nodded and replied, "I can understand how you feel, but I still think we should get tested. If we know we have AIDS, maybe we can get free food parcels from the pastor. That food will help keep us alive longer, because it gives us a more balanced diet."

Duncan shrugged. "We can talk about this later." The idea was still too startling, too horrifying. People all around them were dying of AIDS. Would they be next?

In the following days and months, Alseba and Mama Dolphine faithfully nursed Wilkister, giving her porridge and other things she needed. Duncan knew Alseba hated to care for her ex-rival because of her lingering jealousy.

In spite of this, Alseba told an astonished Duncan that she had been sharing her faith with Wilkister. Unfortunately, the sick woman insisted she was too great a sinner to be saved. "I tell her many times that Jesus came to save everyone, no matter how bad they might be," Alseba said soberly. "But she refuses to believe. Maybe she will wait until it is too late!" Duncan shook his head. He was amazed that Alseba was concerned about the soul of his former wife. Surely it was the power of Jesus!

Six months later, Wilkister died. Alseba actually wiped away tears as she bathed the bony body and dressed her in the expensive dress she had once bought with Duncan's money. Now it hung on her poor emaciated frame. Duncan agreed to let her be buried on his land, though she was not buried behind the house like a real wife would have been. The funeral expenses didn't seem as heavy this time since he had a good job at the mission compound. He had begun working there full-time.

At the wake, he was dry-eyed. When they buried her after a few days, many people wailed, but Alseba only wiped her eyes on her dress sleeve and sniffed loudly. *I can't help but be relieved in a way that she's gone,* thought Duncan. *She will never come back to haunt me again. Yet I am deeply grieved. She never made her peace with God.*

Pastor William had agreed to preach the funeral sermon. He thundered about hell, prepared for those who are not ready to die. He spoke encouragingly of heaven with its rewards. "And now I want to speak to the family," he said, looking directly at Duncan. "God is with us, even when the going gets rough. If you look at the future through eyes of faith, there will be brighter days ahead."

Duncan thought immediately of the question of AIDS. *Eyes of faith,* he mused. *If I have faith that God will be with me no matter what, there is nothing I can fear. Oh God, I give the matter to you. The stress of this worry is too much for me to bear alone.* Some of the pressure of the past few weeks disappeared as he put his faith in God.

But he still didn't want to take the HIV test. *Suppose I have this deathly disease? It would be best not to know.* Even though he felt more peace after the pastor's sermon, the fear of AIDS still lingered.

chapter twenty-four

New Responsibilities

D
URING DUNCAN'S TRIALS, WHILE FACING SO MUCH DEATH, HE HAD almost forgotten about the vision for an orphanage. Although Duncan had been the one to suggest that the nationals oversee it, he had been neglecting to come to the committee meetings. He had too many other things to think about.

Then, one day, Duncan's co-usher, Washington, asked him to come to his house after church for their monthly orphans' meeting. "You are lost nowadays," he told Duncan in the customary manner of saying, "We've missed you."

Duncan nodded. "I've had many problems. Death is too much in my home. But I'm coming."

"Be serious about it," Washington urged him. "You need to start thinking about more things than just death. If you are helping others, this can make you feel happier. Just come this afternoon after church."

"Okay," Duncan consented. "I'll tell Alseba to go home without me and expect me sometime this evening."

At Washington's house they talked about politics and other trivial things until lunch was served. Duncan enjoyed the chicken and *ugali*—chicken was special company fare.

Their meeting began with a word of prayer. When they updated him,

Duncan was amazed at how far the plans had progressed since he had last been to a meeting. "The pastor found sponsors for us in America," Washington informed him.

"Really?" Duncan was surprised. "I thought we had been thinking of doing this without foreign aid."

Another committee member supplied, "We were trying to start a fund, but it grew too slowly. When we told the pastor about our plan, he was very enthusiastic. He had no problem getting people interested." Duncan leaned forward in attention.

Washington went on with the story, "One American supports each orphan. The orphans live with widows who care for them. Using the support money, we buy food for the orphans. The sponsors also provide school fees, uniforms, and schoolbooks."

"But shouldn't we provide our own school?" Duncan suggested. "You know fees are very expensive. NARC, the new political party, says they will give free education to Kenyans. But we cannot know this will happen unless they come into power. Me, I'm not thinking this will happen." Others nodded.

One of the men suggested, "Could we ask our sponsors for money to build a school--not concrete, but mud-walled? We could use some unemployed teachers from our church."

Duncan felt his excitement mounting. "If they are willing to teach for small money, one American could sponsor more children!" The men agreed to move forward with this plan.

When Duncan reached his *dala* in Lela, he met a midwife at the door. She smilingly gestured for him to come inside. "Your wife has delivered a fine son," she told him. Duncan was surprised, but smiled with delight and followed her inside.

"I was not knowing you would give birth today," Duncan told Alseba. "You are okay?"

"Yes, I am going to be fine now," she told him.

Duncan wondered how she made it through the church service. She had said she wasn't feeling well that morning, but hadn't wanted to miss instruction class. He lifted the edge of the blanket and peered at his new son. The infant had a round, puffy face, still light like a *misungu's*. In time, it would become ebony like his own.

"You are naming him what? Ochieng?"

"Yes, he is Ochieng, for he was born in the daytime," Alseba replied. She smiled a very tired smile, but she was as delighted as Duncan with the addition to their family.

Later that week, Pastor William paid a visit to Duncan and Alseba. When the pastor asked what the baby's name was, Alseba told him proudly, "He is called William Ochieng." The pastor tried to hide his grin, but Duncan could tell he was pleased. Pastor William prayed with the young couple with their new responsibility. Duncan felt very blessed. Now he had a son again! Alseba seemed comforted too. She still missed Otieno, and little William would never take his place. But having a new baby helped to fill some of the ache. It helped take their minds off the recent death of Otieno.

That night, however, Duncan tossed and turned in bed. He had been feeling restless for months. Finally he decided to share with his wife. "Alseba, you know sometimes I have trouble sleeping at night."

"Yes, why?" she asked.

"I am thinking of the great salvation I have. But many other people are not knowing Jesus. We are having a church in this area, and the pastor is doing a good work here. But what about other areas?"

Alseba grunted. "You can spread the word of God to people around here," she reminded him.

"But what about people in the Nandi Hills? The Kalinjins need someone to preach for them the true Word of God. I met a man recently at a funeral who works in the Nandi Hills. He said those people are having no churches like ours. Some other Christian churches are there, but they allow polygamy, and many of them are even drunkards. How can they find Jesus?"

"The Kalinjins? Another tribe?" retorted Alseba. "I am not thinking this is a good idea. There are enough Luos you could preach to." After that, she didn't seem inclined to discuss it further. She rolled over in bed and turned her back to him. Soon her even breathing told Duncan she was asleep.

Oh God, why have You given me this burden, but Alseba is not sharing it? He prayed until after midnight, then fell into a restless sleep.

As the months passed, Duncan became increasingly involved in the orphans' school project. Because the cost of their new tin-roofed building was so low and their teachers paid less, they were able to charge minimal school fees. They would begin with a nursery school (kindergarten).

When the first day of school dawned, Duncan climbed onto his bike and went to welcome the new scholars. I have to see that everything is in order, he told himself.

To Washington and Duncan's dismay, many more children came to register than they had enlisted in the orphans' program. "You are not an orphan," Duncan told one girl and her brother. "I know both of your parents, and they are alive. You must go home. This school is only for orphans."

Washington whispered to Duncan, "A lot of parents are sending their children here because of the cheap rates. We need to do research on every child present so we can know if they are true orphans." Duncan agreed.

It took a lot of work, but after a while the school progressed smoothly. Duncan felt fulfilled in his work with the orphan project. Every day found him busy—either in the fields, with bike-taxi work, or at the mission compound. But the restlessness would not leave him. *God, the Kalinjins are dying without salvation,* he would pray. *I know You have called me to go help them. But Alseba doesn't feel the burden with me. And I have no means to go. The church has not sent me.*

A year passed. Duncan's burden didn't diminish; instead it grew. Still Alseba was not excited about the thought of leaving her *dala*—her tribe—for a far-out mission dream. In the meantime, Alseba was baptized with a class of six and radiantly took her place as a full member of the church.

Five more years passed. By now Duncan's family numbered four. Dolphine was their oldest living child, followed by William. Conslata was born the year after Alseba's baptism, and just recently Baby Pius had come to join the family. Although Alseba was happy in the Lord, still she did not feel Duncan's burden for the Kalinjins.

Then one Sunday Pastor William gave an important announcement. "We, the bishop and pastor of this church, have sensed the need for a national pastor. We want to choose this new church leader soon. The way we have ordination is by drawing a lot. There will be no politicking involved, for man will not choose your new leader, but God." Duncan was shocked at the news. A stunned silence pervaded the auditorium.

Afterwards he told Washington, "I had no idea they were thinking of choosing a pastor from among us. Do you think this means Pastor William wants to leave us?"

"No," Washington assured him. "You heard him say he needs a helper. He will stay in Kenya." Duncan shook his head, not quite believing it. All other pastors ordained national leaders before they left the country.

When he and Alseba talked about this, she wondered what would happen if someone were chosen from an area other than Lela. "If someone from Kabongo is ordained, they will take the church over there. It will be too far for us to walk," she worried.

"Pastor William said no one is taking the church," Duncan reminded her. "It will stay here. He said the white pastor will not leave. But I guess we don't know these things until they happen."

Alseba nodded. Then she posed another question. "Do you think you will be chosen?"

"I can't know something that is happening in the future," Duncan reminded her. "But with the burden I am having for the Kalinjin tribe, becoming a pastor seems like it would be the first step. Later we could move away to take the Gospel to them. I would like to be a pastor, but I don't know the will of God."

Alseba gave a start. "I am not feeling called to go to the Nandis. And I could never be a pastor's wife!"

Duncan hung his head. "I was such a sinner. I know I can never be good enough to be a pastor either. Maybe it will never be possible because of my sinful past. But I know I can still be a witness for God." His voice broke. "Let's commit this to the Lord.

"Oh God," he prayed, "Please hear our prayer. We have heard of the ordination our bishop and pastor want to do in our church. Be with the one you have chosen. Help us to feel peace about it. If you have called us to spread your word to another tribe, make us willing to do your work." He sighed.

Alseba was too shy to pray aloud, but together they said, "Amen."

Then Alseba glanced at Duncan. "What about the AIDS test?" she changed the subject. "You are very thin, and I seem to pick up every sickness that goes around. Do you want to take the test? If we tested positive, we could get free food parcels for a balanced diet."

Duncan's stomach churned. *Why must she bring this up now? I have enough to worry about.* Aloud he said, "I don't want to do the test. But I will pray about it. If it's the right thing to do, I want be willing."

As Duncan waited on the evening meal, he prayed silently, *Dear Lord, please give me peace. Help me not to worry about the diagnosis of an HIV test. Also, about my burden for the Nandis—either take it away, or help me to fulfill it. May Alseba also yearn to win those souls for You. About the ordination …* Duncan's heart pounded, and he swallowed hard. *Help me not to fear about who will be chosen. In some ways, I want to be a pastor. Yet I don't feel worthy.*

When Alseba brought in his evening *ugali*, he invited her to eat with him. "It's just Luo culture that forbids men to eat with women," he reminded her. "Let's eat our meal together." Shyly she sat down with him and ate. Dolphine, William, and Nina sat on the floor with their bowls of *ugali* and *sakumu*. Baby Pius was asleep.

The calmness of peace stole over Duncan as a Voice seemed to say, *No matter what happens, I will go with you. Don't be afraid.* As Duncan trusted his God, he found strength.

chapter twenty-five

A New Pastor

THE CRISP MORNING CARRIED A PROMISE OF THE TYPICAL SOARING temperatures of dry season. "This is the Sunday the church will choose a national leader," Duncan reminded Alseba, who was bent over tying baby Pius to her back with a cloth. She straightened up and balanced her Bible on her head—a handy way to carry it for the long walk to church.

"Are you nervous?" she asked her husband. "Anyone can be ordained, even you."

Duncan gazed at the woman he loved. "Yes. I'm not knowing what will happen. And you're right, it could be me. But I'm willing to do anything for the Lord. Are you?" He took William and Nina by the hands and began walking beside Alseba. Six-year-old Dolphine tagged along behind, carrying Alseba's basket.

After a long pause, Alseba replied, "Yes, I'm willing. I am willing to be a pastor's wife. But only that. Not a missionary's wife."

Duncan winced. *My, she can be stubborn.* He remembered how she had balked at becoming saved so long ago. *Oh Lord, if You really want me to be a missionary for You to the Kalinjins, please persuade Alseba. Give her the same vision.* Duncan had been praying this prayer for so many years. He sighed. *Will it ever be answered?*

When they reached the church, it was packed full of people. Nobody wanted to miss this service, when a national leader would be chosen. Duncan remembered how the pastor had cautioned them against using church politics to vie for the position. "God is the One who will choose our leader—the new pastor will not be chosen by man's wisdom," the pastor had said.

Duncan walked inside and sat down in his usual spot at the end of the third bench. He fidgeted on the seat, concerned about the outcome of this service. In a previous service, all the members had filed into the back rooms to suggest the names of men they felt qualified to as pastor. No one would know the names of those in the lot until this morning.

In all the other churches, someone is appointed or elected to be pastor. I wonder how this will be different, Duncan wondered. *The pastor said God is the One who will do the choosing. He said man will not have his finger in it.*

He watched soberly as the bishop went up to the pulpit. Apparently one man would be chosen from a group. "The ones in the lot are Washington, Fred, Meshack, and Duncan," the bishop told the congregation soberly.

Duncan felt a jolt that was almost electric. His stunned face met Alseba's calm one across the aisle. Why doesn't she look more nervous? Duncan found himself drawing on her strength even though she sat halfway across the building. But he still felt anxious and inadequate.

Oh Lord, he prayed, *I'm ready for anything You ask me to do. Only give me strength. I feel like I can't do this. I was such a terrible sinner before my salvation. How can I ever be a pastor? Don't make me do this, God!*

Then he felt a gentle, sweet peace, and a Voice seemed to say, "My grace is sufficient for everything I ask of you." Duncan felt his fears dissipate.

He watched Pastor William take four new Luo Bibles. The pastor put a slip of paper in one of them. Someone took the Bibles into the back room to shuffle them. They were shuffled again and again, until Duncan was sure even the pastor and bishop had lost track of which Bible the paper was in.

The Bibles were placed on a table in front of the room. Duncan and Alseba sat on the front bench with the other couples in the lot. Duncan watched breathlessly as Fred arose to choose his book. *May as well pick up my book now,* Duncan thought. He stepped up and hesitantly took a Bible. Next, Meshack chose a book. Lastly, Washington slowly took the remaining Bible.

Fred's Bible was opened first. There was no paper inside, and Duncan heard Fred's wife give an audible gasp of relief. A murmur grew in the church as people discussed the proceedings with their seatmates.

Next the bishop opened Duncan's book. His heart hammered wildly. Is this the moment? he wondered. But the book was empty! Duncan felt all the air escaping his lungs. Beside him, Alseba gave thumbs up without thinking, then hid her face with embarrassment. Duncan had never felt such relief, but he also felt a little let down at the same time. *I thought I might be the next pastor,* he thought.

Washington's book was opened next, and there was the little white paper. The congregation buzzed now. Washington would be the new pastor! Nothing like this had ever happened before that anyone could remember.

When the time came for testimonies, many people gave God the glory for the extraordinary event they had witnessed. "Truly I can see that God was doing the choosing," said Mama Dolphine when she stood up to testify. "In other churches, pastors are not chosen in this way. We can know there is nothing humans did to ordain this man. Praise the Lord!"

"Amen!" echoed the congregation. After the service, Pastor William gave Duncan the new Luo Bible to keep. But his new possession didn't help him overcome his sense of loss. *It would have been so nice to be ordained if I am going to be a missionary,* Duncan thought.

All the same, Duncan welcomed his brother Washington wholeheartedly. "May God bless you!" he said as he greeted him. "I will pray for you and support you."

As Duncan walked home with Alseba, he was unusually silent, trying to wrestle with the conflicting emotions within him. Finally, Alseba asked, "How are you feeling? Are you happy to be free of this work?" She continued to possess a peace Duncan envied.

"I am happy," Duncan replied. "But I … I thought I would be … well, I thought if I would be a pastor, I could preach to the people in Nandi Hills."

"Heh," breathed Alseba sharply. "You don't have to be a pastor in order to spread the Word of God to other places. But I still don't understand why you think you must go to the Nandi Hills to witness. There are many unsaved people here in Kano Plains."

Alseba, don't you see?" Duncan asked earnestly. "Oh, I've been praying for so long that you might understand and feel the same burden I do. We cannot go in a divided way. We must be together in feeling the need to reach out to the Kalinjins."

Alseba looked distressed. "The Kalinjins? Duncan, why did God give you a burden for them? They would never listen to a Luo. They think themselves so far above us in every way."

"But the Good News is greater than any tribal differences," Duncan argued. "Whether I were a Kalinjin, Kamba, or Masai, I would want to be told the Good News so I could be saved. I don't think it would matter to me who brought this news to me, even if he were a Luo."

Alseba sighed and shook her head. Her mouth was in the familiar straight line that bespoke her stubbornness. Duncan held his peace as well and prayed about his burden the rest of the way home.

That evening, Alseba brought up the subject of the HIV test once more. "I think we should get tested," she said. "Baby Pius is sick all the time, it seems, and you are very thin. Even me, I'm sick a lot. Even if we don't test positive, at least we will know."

"I'm thinking we probably have the virus," Duncan finally admitted. "I have thought so for years, but I didn't want to take the test. It's like knowing I will die soon."

"Remember the various help projects the church has for people who have AIDS," Alseba reminded him. "Not only would they give us food parcels, but if our blood count were low enough, they could give us antiretroviral drugs."

"Antiretroviral drugs?" Duncan asked. "I'm not thinking I know about that."

"It is a very expensive drug given to certain people if they are low in blood," Alseba replied. "Once a person starts on this drug, they must keep on or risk a terrible setback and death. If they keep taking the drug, it will add them days and keep them healthy."

"That is very good," Duncan said. "I hope we will not need anything like that. But the first step is to be tested. Let's go together to Russia Hospital on Thursday."

Alseba looked shocked. "I've been wanting you to do this for many years," she reminded him. "What made you change your mind?"

Duncan wanted to say, *To show I'm not as stubborn as you,* but he knew that would never do. Instead he replied, "You have persuaded me well. I am now seeing it as you are." Alseba nodded, but he could tell she knew he wasn't saying everything.

Duncan hoped he would sleep that night. Not only did he have the ordination to think about, but now he was dreading the HIV test. *Do we have AIDS?* he couldn't help worrying. *If we do, will we need to go on antiretroviral drugs?*

chapter twenty-six

The Word Goes Forth

In the days that followed, Duncan struggled with deep discouragement. As he hoed the maize, he again wondered, Why wasn't I ordained? Am I not worth as much to God as Washington? Did God make a mistake? Shouldn't I be a pastor if He is calling me to be a missionary? Duncan didn't want to admit it, but deep down inside he would have liked the prestige and position of being a pastor. *Even if I know I'm not worthy,* he reminded himself, whacking out a thistle with his hoe.

As Duncan moved on to the next row, he thought again of the HIV test they would take Thursday. Great dread filled his heart. *Oh God, please help me to test negative! I don't want to get thin and die. We used to call it chira, but now we know it's AIDS.*

Once more a Voice seemed to say, "My grace is sufficient for you. Don't worry. You are Mine no matter what happens."

Duncan stooped over to pull away some weeds from the ground he had dug up. *God, life is so difficult! I have so many worries. I'm still trying to accept that I was not ordained. At the same time, I've agreed to do the HIV test. Not only that, but my heart continues to be troubled that Alseba doesn't want to go with me to Nandi Hills.* Then Duncan felt a peace stealing over his heart. It helped just to tell God all about it—to realize He was in control.

Thursday came before Duncan was ready. Alseba left the children with Mama Dolphine and walked with Duncan out to the road. Duncan didn't say a word the whole way out. His stomach churned with anxiety.

Duncan flagged down a public vehicle, and off they went to Kisumu. After they alighted at the station, the couple walked to Russia Hospital. There they met with a counselor, who asked them some personal questions. Then a lab technician took their blood samples. "Come back next Monday for your results," he told them.

On the way to the bus stage, Duncan confided to Alseba, "I don't know how I can wait until next week. I wish I knew now!"

"Me too," Alseba replied, her voice trembling. Duncan looked at her hard. *Alseba was the one pushing to take the test, but she looks every bit as frightened as I am,* he pondered. Somehow this made him feel better.

But before they set out to get the results, something remarkable happened. Alseba had brought in the *ugali* and *sakumu* for their supper, and they sat down to eat together. Then she said, "Duncan, I had a dream last night. In the dream I saw you and myself with our four children in a hut made of very red soil. We lived on a steep mountainside. Our fields were on such a steep slope, it made me fear I was going to fall down when I went to weed. Just before I woke up, I saw you preaching to some Kalinjins. Then I knew we were in Nandi Hills."

Duncan gaped at her. *Where did this dream come from?* he wondered. *Dreams are very significant to us Luos.*

Alseba went on, "I knew this was God's way of telling me I was wrong to be so stubborn about going with you to Nandi Hills. If this is God's call to you, I know He has called me too."

Duncan went over and took her in his arms in a rare display of affection. "Oh Alseba, I'm so glad God answered my prayer!" he breathed. "He is faithful!"

In the glow of this victory, Duncan went alone to Kisumu to get the results of their HIV test. It cost too much for them to go together again. As he traveled, he couldn't help but praise the Lord that Alseba was now willing to go with Him to the Kalinjins. Perhaps it would take time, but Duncan was sure she would also feel the same burden he did.

But when he got the test results, his heart sank. Both of them were HIV positive. His heart withered and fluttered down to the soles of his flip-flops. Even though he received counseling, he couldn't seem to absorb it because of the "death sentence" he had just received.

Oh God, he groaned in his heart. *This is too much. I thought You were on my side because of Alseba's victory. But now—do You really love me?* Depressed, Duncan's steps drooped as he walked down the familiar path from Lela to his home.

He thought back to the day so long ago when he and Mama Dolphine had walked this path for the first time. God's perfect plan had given him a loving mother and led him to find the Lord. But where was this God? Was this the same God who spared the life of the missionary when the angry mob wanted to lynch him? Was this the same God who helped him get released from Kodiga prison? Did this God allow them to test HIV positive?

He softly entered the house where Alseba was crocheting. She seemed to read the dejection on his face. "We tested positive?" she asked unnecessarily.

"Yes," Duncan replied. He plopped into the one-armed chair and buried his face in his hands. *God, where are You?* his heart pled.

Alseba touched him. He raised his head as she said, "Duncan, don't be sad. Remember we have the Lord. And just because you know you are HIV positive doesn't change anything. It is good that we know. Now we can get free food parcels. If are low in blood, we can perhaps take antiretroviral drugs."

"I don't care about any of those things," Duncan mumbled. "I just know I am going to die."

"No, you're not going to die," Alseba protested. "People with the HIV virus can often live long lives before they get full-blown AIDS. Remember what the counselor told us? We haven't necessarily passed it down to all our children, although I suspect Baby Pius has the virus. If we get a balanced diet, our lives can be prolonged."

Duncan just shook his head. "I know what you say is true, but it is still a terrible thing to know." He walked out of the house and went to the *shamba*. (field) He wasn't sure what he was going to do out there, since he didn't even carry his hoe.

Duncan wandered about aimlessly, trying to pray, but unable to do more than just groan. He came back in the evening for supper, his heart still full of turmoil.

For weeks, Duncan battled depression. He didn't feel like working, but when he just sat in the house, he felt as if he was plunged into a bottomless pit. Alseba seemed concerned, yet unsure how to help him.

Pastor William came to visit Duncan after he had missed three Sundays of church. "What's wrong, Duncan?" he asked. "Alseba has told me you are discouraged."

"Pastor, Alseba and I took the HIV test," he replied. "Here are the results, *e-e*," he showed him. "I feel very discouraged about this. This tells me I am going to die."

"Not necessarily," the pastor replied. "People with HIV can often live long lives, especially when helped with antiretroviral drugs. This is just a new program. Have you heard of it?" he asked.

"Yes, Alseba told me," Duncan replied. "I didn't consent to take the test for years, even though she wanted to. She wanted to benefit from free food parcels."

"Well," said the pastor, "That's not a good reason to take the test. But since you felt free to show me the results of your test, we can give you the parcels. I'd be more than happy to help you in this way." Duncan felt his spirits lifting at the pastor's kindness.

"Thank you," he replied.

After that, Duncan slowly began to feel more useful. He had struggled for so long with wondering if God really needed him. He apparently wasn't called to be a pastor, and he also carried the dread HIV virus. But at the next reorganization, the church elected him as an adult Sunday school teacher. Duncan enjoyed preparing the lessons, although he often felt nervous when presenting them.

Then, one Sunday, the pastor made a startling announcement. "The mission board has seen the need for outreach into other areas—to other tribes." Duncan held his breath. "We feel like the time has come to send some of our people to the Kalinjin tribe." Duncan exhaled. He could not believe his ears. *Was this what the Lord was preparing me for all along? Is this why He gave me this burden?* "We want to know if there are any volunteers among you to go to this important work. We are open to having two families go, and one of them would be commissioned to preach."

The church began to buzz as people discussed this news with each other. *Nothing like this has ever been heard of before!* Duncan mused. *But God called me many years ago. Now is my chance. I must volunteer. Even Alseba will agree now.* Duncan felt his depression leaving him.

"I think God is calling us to go share the Word with the Kalinjin tribe!" Duncan enthused to Alseba on the way home. "It seems God does want to use me! I was so disappointed after the ordination, but it looks like God had another plan for me."

"Yes, God called you a long time ago. I wonder why He didn't wait to call you until He was ready to put His plan into action? Why did He give you this burden so long ago?" she wondered.

"Well, maybe He needed time to convince you," Duncan smiled to her.

"Yes. How stubborn I was! But now I feel the same burden you do."

Duncan was very excited, yet he knew it wouldn't be easy to leave his clan, his tribe, and his church. There would be many adjustments to make, but God would be with them, for He had called them! Together they would face the trials that came their way.

Out loud, Duncan said, "I don't think Mama Dolphine will be very happy that we want to move to the Nandis."

Alseba nodded gravely. "But she will give us her blessing even if she doesn't understand. Don't you think?"

"Yes," Duncan replied.

Pastor William, the bishop, and the mission board accepted Duncan as a volunteer to go to the Nandi Hills as a missionary. Washington also volunteered, eliminating the need to commission a pastor for this work.

The morning Duncan's family moved away was a painful one of parting. "Good-bye, Mama Dolphine," he said, his voice trembling. "Thank you for all you did for me. I will never be able to repay you for taking me off the streets and giving me a home."

"It was because of love," Mama reminded him. "I'm sending this love to go with you." She wiped a tear on her sleeve. "God will also go with you, and give you His peace."

Duncan swallowed hard, then turned to Jaduong. *Will I ever see him again?* he wondered. "Jaduong, thank you for making a home for me." He shook the old man's hand. Only by the grace of God had Duncan been able to forgive his foster father for not accepting him. Jaduong only grunted and used his cane to shuffle over his favorite mango tree.

Pius was still working in Nairobi; Duncan didn't know when he would see him again. It was too bad he couldn't tell his foster brother good-bye.

After all the farewells had been said, Duncan put the two chests of clothing they owned in the back of the pastor's Cruiser. Washington's family's belongings were already there. They tied a few pieces of furniture on top of the vehicle. *It will be hard to start out with so little,* Duncan mused. *At least the church will be supporting us—paying our rent and a few hundred shillings a week to help with food.*

Pastor William asked the clan to gather in a circle with Washington's family for a word of prayer. "Oh God," he prayed, "Thank You for calling Duncan and Washington with their families to serve You in Nandi Hills. Now be with them and bless them. May they win many souls for the Kingdom. In Jesus' Name."

Everyone joined in on the "Amen." And so Duncan, Alseba, and their family left the clan and their tribe to begin a new life with the Kalinjins. They drove away to a new life and new beginnings. Duncan had felt the Lord's hand on him through the years. He knew his God would continue to be with him, no matter what the future held.

A note from the author

Deliverance for Duncan is based on many true happenings in Kenya. However, Duncan himself is a totally fictitious character. The events in this book did not all happen to one person. For example, a street boy did beg for money and was given bread in exchange for his glue. But this was not the same person who stole money from the missionaries. The beating actually did happen, although there was one more missionary beaten than the story depicts. Duncan's involvement in it is something I construed for my story plot.

The pictures on the cover and inside the book do not represent actual people written about in the book. Rather, they are random photos of life in Kenya to make African life more real to you. I hope this book can give you a picture of how Kenya really is, through the eyes of one from the Luo tribe, and that it can be a blessing to you.